Advance Praise for
The Baritone Wore Chiffon

"Reading this book is like a 12 step program, except in step 9, the author should apologize to everyone concerned."
Tony Robbins, motivational speaker

"If I catch you inside my garage again, I'll shoot you. I MEAN it! And put those *Playboys* back!"
John Rutter, orthodontist, Great Falls, Montana

"...along the way, he creates an enchanting Mitford-Bizarro world...warm and fuzzy in the way that a rabid raccoon is warm and fuzzy..."
Logan Askew, Attorney

"I would cheerfully pay Schweizer's funeral expenses at any time."
His Grace, Lord Horatio "Wiggles" Biggerstaff, retired bishop

"This novel, like his first, could have been prevented by just one good English teacher..."
Sandy Cavanah, college professor

"This is not a book to be tossed aside lightly. It should be thrown with great force!"
Liz Trice, college student

"Publishers and critics have long ignored the importance of shoddy writing in the detective genre of the mid to late twentieth century. This landmark book gives mediocrity the place it deserves."
Anthony Hatteberg, eighth-grade genius

"He [Schweizer] uses the English language in the way a baby seal hunter uses a club..."
Fred May, bank president and incidental character

"It even looks like a real book, with pages and print and everything. The disguise is extremely clever considering the contents."
Dr. Robert Sivley, forensic psychologist

"Yeah, I read it. So what?"
Billy Hicks, lawn care professional

"GUILTY, BY GOD! And you're going away for a long time!"
The Hon. James G. Adams, judge

The Baritone Wore Chiffon
A Liturgical Mystery
Copyright ©2004 by Mark Schweizer

Illustrations by Jim Hunt
www.jimhuntillustration.com

Published by
St. James Music Press
www.sjmp.com
P.O. Box 1009
Hopkinsville, KY 42241-1009

ISBN 0-9721211-3-7

Printed in the United States of America

1st Printing February, 2004

Acknowledgements

Richard Shephard
John Schrecker
Sandy Cavanah
Kristen Linduff
Drs. Karen and Ken Dougherty
All the many anonymous writers of bad similes that
never failed to inspire and of which I borrowed more than a few.

The Baritone Wore Chiffon

A Liturgical Mystery

by Mark Schweizer
illustrations by Jim Hunt

For Lindy, who taught us all
the true meaning of coulrophobia.

Can't sleep, clowns will eat me...
Can't sleep, clowns will eat me...
Can't sleep, clowns will eat me...

Prelude

Prelude

I sat down and looked lovingly at the typewriter sitting on the desk, running my fingers across the worn keys and remembering when I first saw it offered in an on-line auction. Raymond Chandler's 1939 Underwood No. 5. The very typewriter that had been used to write *The High Window, Trouble Is My Business, Goldfish,* and a host of other hard-boiled detective stories in the 40's and 50's. I put a piece of paper into the carriage and, with a feeling of reverence, clicked the return until the edge of the paper appeared behind the hammers and inched across the roller. Just to see what it felt like, I opened a copy of *Trouble Is My Business* and copied a passage onto the bright, new piece of bond.

I called him from a phone booth. The voice that answered was fat. It wheezed softly, like the voice of a man who had just won a pie-eating contest.

I chuckled with delight, knowing that I had typed the same words on the same machine as Raymond Chandler had some forty years before. I indulged myself a second time, this time from memory.

From thirty feet away, she looked like a lot of class. From ten feet away, she looked like something made up to be seen from thirty feet away.

I had finished my first work, *The Alto Wore Tweed,* before Christmas and was ready to begin my second opus. As an organist and choir director, I was pretty good; as a detective, I was excellent; but as an author, I was without peer. Or so said many of my friends. Those are the exact words. "Without peer."

I put a new piece of paper into the typewriter, rolled it forward and, with slightly trembling fingers, typed

The Baritone Wore Chiffon
Chapter One

I walked over to the kitchen and collected my beer and sandwich. Then, with the ghost of Philip Marlowe, Chandler's hard driving private-eye, looking over my shoulder, I started typing.

It was a dark and stormy night: dark, because the sun had just set like a giant flaming hen squatting upon her unkempt nest that was the gritty urban streets; stormy, because the weather had rolled in like an angry fat man driving his Rascal into a Ryan's Steak House and then finding out that the "all you can eat" dessert bar had an out-of-order frozen yogurt machine. Suddenly, a shot rang out, as shots are wont to do. No, I decided. Not a shot. Just the backfire of a too old car with bad gas, a problem that I could easily identify with.

I sat in my chair, my feet up on the desk, the rain from my shoes dripping onto the blotter, mixing with the dried ink and swirling into what looked like the "naked trapeze girl with a top hat" on the Rorschach test--a test which, at this point in time, I'm not sure I could have passed with a C minus. I had a drink. Then another. If I had put away the second the way I had the first, I probably wouldn't have heard the rap on the door. "C'mon in," I grumbled. It had been a bad day.

She came in like a centipede with 98 missing legs. Attractive? Sure. But though I wasn't interested, a sawbuck is a sawbuck, and that's what it'd cost her to bend my ear. I lit up a cigar in anticipation.

"I'm Kit," she said. She had a hungry look, the kind you get from not eating for a few days. "I'm looking for a job. I'm a Girl-Friday."

"Come back tomorrow," I said. "I'm as beat as two-day old meringue."

"Have you no shame?" Meg asked, shaking her head and dropping my prose onto the desk with disdain. "This is quite possibly the worst thing ever written. And I'm including your past efforts. I'm embarrassed for you."

"I am secure in my literary prowess. I am a fine writer."

"You are mistaken. You are bad. Truly bad. And I may have to stop you."

I read back over the uneven text. For me, style and content were of secondary importance. The old-fashioned look of the type, the clatter of the well-worn keys and the way the paper curled over the platen were reason enough to write. Good or bad. Okay. Bad. Still, I thought that Megan Farthing at least, being my significant other, should stick up for my hackneyed efforts. I could use a little positive reinforcement.

"You are positively terrible. Please stop now, before I do something which I may regret but for which the literary world will have cause to thank me."

I admit it. I'm an incurable Chandler fan. I put *Trouble Is My Business* back on the shelf and thumbed open *The Long Goodbye*, my current re-read.

"Then her hands dropped and jerked at something and the robe she was wearing came open and underneath it she was as naked as September Morn but a darn sight less coy."

As they say up here in the hills, "Man, that's real good writin'."

Chapter 1

"Hayden, supper's almost ready," Meg called. She had been in the kitchen for an hour or so, making a trip into the den every once in a while to bring me a beer and to check up on how I was coming with my new masterpiece. Seeing as Lent was four days away and I was trying to garner some piety, I was listening to the *St. Luke Passion* of Penderecki. It's not an easy piece to listen to, but if you can get through all ninety minutes, you'll be more than ready for Lent. In fact, Lent will be a piece of cake. It's the musical equivalent of having your wisdom teeth pulled without Novocain. The fact that I was giving up beer for forty days also had a bearing on my selection. I wanted Meg to suffer as much as I. She was giving up needlepoint. I pointed out that this was hardly a challenge.

"You're missing the spirit of Lent, Hayden. You give up something so that when you'd be working at that activity, you can meditate or do some reading instead. Something that enriches your life and your spiritual existence."

"Nope. Lent is about suffering. And the quicker you accept it, the easier it'll be. It's all about suffering and guilt," I said smugly, turning up the volume on the stereo and feeling my fillings give way.

The den was actually an old log cabin, measuring twenty by twenty, complete with a loft that I had incorporated into the overall design of the house. My house suited me very well and fit snugly into the two hundred acres in the middle of the Blue Ridge Mountains that I called home. The kitchen, in contrast with the rest of the house, and due to Meg's insistence, was totally modern, the only nod toward rusticity being the stone fireplace and the exposed beams which held up the second floor. The entire building cost a pretty penny, but pretty pennies were what I had. A whole lot of them.

"Do we have to listen to that god-awful wailing?" Meg asked, her face slightly askew.

"Yes, dear. Lent is upon us. And the Passion is a twentieth century masterpiece."

"What about Bach? Or some medieval chant or maybe a cantata? Even Albinoni? This is just painful."

"All in good time, my pretty. Ash Wednesday is four days away. We haven't even begun to suffer."

I am, by vocation, a police detective, by avocation, a church musician, but my fortune was made with the phone company thanks to a little invention that paid off handsomely and which Meg, also my investment counselor, has brokered into quite a tidy sum. I actually don't *have* to work, but I enjoy it, so every day I make my way into St. Germaine, a quaint little town up in the mountains of North Carolina, where I am the Chief Police Detective, and straight to my table at The Slab Cafe. At least for my morning coffee.

On Sundays it's off to the downtown square and St. Barnabas Episcopal Church where I am the resident organist and choirmaster. It's a nice job and one I would probably treat a bit more reverently if I actually needed the salary. As it is, I put the money back into the music fund. And it's a fair use of my first two college degrees. It was my third that got me into police work.

"Well, you've chased the boys outside. I doubt they'll be back for a while."

"The boys" Meg was referring to were Baxter and Archimedes, who usually have the run of the house. Baxter is a Burmese Mountain Dog, not even six months old and already huge. I had given him to Meg for a Christmas present, but he'd ended up living out here. Meg, who lived in town with her mother, didn't have the room, and Baxter had the makings of a terrific watchdog – even at his tender age.

Archimedes is an owl. He showed up about five months ago on my windowsill. I fed him for a few weeks, and he gradually became reasonably tame. We feed him, but he's a wild owl and we don't pick him up. I tried letting him step onto my hand, but his talons went right to the bone and I still have the scars. He has a window with an automatic opener which he learned to activate without much trouble, and now he comes and goes as he pleases, knowing there's always a dead mouse or squirrel waiting for him in the kitchen. I buy the frozen rodents by the case from Kent Murphee, the coroner in Boone. Where he gets them, I have no idea, and I don't ask.

The sopranos hit a particularly high and harsh note.

"If Lent is going to be like this, you can kiss me good-bye till Easter." Meg was getting a bit perturbed. And she was beginning to develop a twitch in her left eye.

"OK. I'll turn it off for now, but just know that I'll be listening to the rest of it later on. It's no good suffering unless someone knows it. You have to have an audience."

"Oh brother!"

"And, by the way, giving up needlepoint for Lent is hardly a sacrifice. You don't even needlepoint any more. What's your real plan? To give up watching your mother needlepoint?"

"Oops, I've got to go," Meg said, suddenly looking at her watch and racing for the door. "I forgot that I have to pick Mother up at her book club."

"What about supper?"

"Put it in the fridge. I'll be back in an hour and I expect some decent dinner music. Till then, have a miserable Lent."

"Yes, that's the idea," I called after her.

Kit was waiting in my office when I came in.

"I need a job. I need a job bad."

Her grammar wasn't great, but then grammar never is. I really didn't need a Girl-Friday, but I figured that if I could get the client to cover the cost, I'd be that much ahead.

I'm an L.D. That's Liturgy Detective, duly licensed by the diocese of North Carolina and appointed by the Bishop's Council on Physical Fitness. The International Congress of Church Musicians had me on retainer, but since the case of The Alto Wore Tweed, things had been a little slow around the office. Polite, church-going people had apparently shunned me. It seemed like there still wasn't room for people of all fashions in ecumenical society. My latest case involved a family of Full Gospel Raccoons that was wreaking havoc on an Episcopalian Mobile Home Park. I couldn't tell yet if they were proselytizing or just eating the garbage, but it was just a matter of time.

"Sprechen sie hard-boiled?" I asked.

"You dumb palooka, get your nose out of the eel juice before I stuff that stogie down your mush. I'm a dame that needs some bim." She grinned.

She was good all right. Maybe too good. She could speak hard-boiled better than most flatfeet.

"The sucker with the snoozle poured a slug but before he could drift, a couple of ginks showed him the shiv and he hopped in a boiler. It was eggs in the coffee."

"Yeah. OK. You'll be fine. Now hustle your pins down to Marilyn and tell her to order me a sandwich.

I'll call you when I need you."

It was gonna be a long day.

The phone was ringing as I stepped out of the shower on Sunday morning.

"Hayden Konig," I said.

"Hayden, how are you? It's about time you were up and about." I recognized the voice right away.

"Ah, Hugh, how are things in England?"

"Terribly busy, as usual. I just called to give you a heads up."

"About what?"

"You're going to be getting a call from one of our city's finest. It seems that there's been a murder at the Minster."

Hugh Kirkby was a priest and canon at York Minster.

"So why call me?" I asked.

"He was a choir member – a songman – who was over here on a fellowship from North Carolina. Raleigh to be exact. Anyway, the Dean wanted someone from the colonies involved – strictly as a courtesy – so I suggested the Minster Police contact you. It would be a free trip across. And some cash to boot."

"That sounds like a deal. Do I actually have to do anything?"

"Just solve the crime and make us all look good."

"That should be no problem at all," I said.

"Great. We'll clear it with the Home Office and get all your papers in order. Otherwise you won't get paid."

"By all means," I said agreeably.

"Get a flight on Thursday. See you soon."

Monday morning found me down at the Slab. I opened the door and saw Nancy and Dave already holding our table. Nancy Parsky is the other full-timer on the force and can only be described as "an efficient law enforcement professional." At least to her face. Dave Vance answers the phones, has a crush on Nancy, and only works about twenty hours a week.

"Mornin', Pete," I called, as I walked over to the coffee pot and poured myself a mug.

Pete Moss is my old roommate from college, the mayor of St. Germaine, and the owner of the Slab Cafe.

"Good mornin', yourself. Grab your chair. I'll be out in a minute with some grub."

I pulled up a chair across from Nancy. She had just taken her notepad from the breast pocket of her freshly starched shirt. Nancy was the only one of the three of us who wore a uniform and the only one to carry a gun. Dave almost always wore a Land's End ensemble. This time of year, I'm usually in a flannel shirt and jeans – not to mention a jacket. The weather in February in the mountains of North Carolina can be downright bitter. We hadn't had a lot of snow since January began, but the cold hung on like a kitten on a pair of corduroy pants.

"What's on the agenda?" asked Dave.

I deferred to Nancy with an upraised eyebrow.

"Nothing much," said Nancy, checking her notebook. "It's another cold week, and all the various and sundry ne'er-do-wells have holed up for the duration of the winter. It's my new theory."

"Sort of like criminal hibernation," said Dave.

"Exactly."

"Maybe you should write a thesis on your hypothesis," I quipped. "They'd be happy to hear about it in Alaska, since they obviously have no crime at all ten months out of the year."

"What about Antarctica?" said Dave. "That's even colder than Alaska."

Nancy rolled her eyes. "Dave, there are no actual people in Antarctica. Just scientists and penguins."

"What about seals?" Pete had just come up to the table, bringing some country ham biscuits and a big bowl of grits. "I'm pretty sure there're seals."

"How 'bout when they kill them baby seals to make fur coats?" It was Noylene Fabergé, Pete's new waitress. "I'd sure call that a crime." She paused. "Unless I had me one of them coats."

"Forget about those seals, Noylene," I said. "You should be worrying about those little polyesters slaughtered on the ice by harpoon wielding Eskimo evangelists in lime-green leisure snowsuits."

Dave choked back half a laugh and covered it with a mouthful of coffee.

Noylene looked shocked. "No kiddin'? Well, I'm writin' a letter. My congressman's gonna hear about them Eskimos." She was shaking her head as she left the table.

"You shouldn't do that to Noylene," Pete said, pulling up a chair and making himself at home. "Have some grits."

"Anyway," continued Nancy, spooning some grits onto her plate as if nothing had happened. "It's shaping up to be a very slow week. So unless we have a major crime spree, it would be a good time for a vacation."

"Speaking of which," I said. "I'll be going over to England for a few days to help in a murder investigation."

"It's probably not cold enough over there," said Pete through a mouthful of ham biscuit.

"I guess not. There was a choir member killed in York Minster. A guy from Raleigh over there on a fellowship, so they want me to be on hand."

"And they're calling you to come over?" asked Pete. I could tell he was impressed. "Are you that well known?"

"I know a few folks over there and they want an American involved in the investigation. Politics I think."

"Can I call the newspaper and get something in there about it?" asked Pete. As mayor, he was always looking for any chance of publicity. "It'll be a great local interest story. 'St. Germaine Cop Called To Assist Scotland Yard'"

"Sure," I said. "It's fine with me. I'll e-mail you the details."

"Great!" said Pete. "I'll call it in this afternoon."

"How about me?" asked Nancy, hopefully. "I'll be happy to go. I want to be in the paper, too."

"Nope. You have to stay here and keep watch over your hypothesis."

Chapter 2

"Marilyn", I called, looking carefully at the sandwich delivery boy. "How am I gonna pay for this?"

She sauntered in. Marilyn had an hourglass figure with an extra twenty minutes thrown in for good measure. And she made a good cup of coffee.

"There's $1.57 left in petty cash." She smiled politely and shrugged her shoulders as she tap-danced coyly back to her desk.

The delivery boy frowned. "I'll just put it on your tab."

"Make sure you add a nice tip for yourself," I called after him as he left. "And close the door after you."

He was a nice kid. He'd done some work for me before and he was interested in learning the business. That is - until he'd seen the down side. In the L.D. business, it's not all sopranos wearing red.

Finishing my lunch, I reached for a stogie and a cup of joe. Suddenly a shot rang out. A woman screamed. No--Marilyn screamed, but I was used to that. A dog barked. A phone rang. Marilyn screamed again. I lit my cigar and looked up.

There she was, the bishop's new personal trainer and executive secretary, standing in the doorway, an imaginary zephyr blowing softly through her hair, and all of a sudden I remembered why it was good to be the bishop. Her name, if I remembered correctly - and I don't think I'd forget, was Roxanne--otherwise known as Rocki. Rocki Pilates.

"I have some big news from the bishop," she said

in a low voice. "Can we be alone?"

"Marilyn," I yelped, my voice going up a dimin-
ished seventh. "Take your lunch ... NOW!"

"But I'm not hun-..."

The slam of the door cut off anything Marilyn
had to say, but somehow I suspected she'd be listening
intently on the other side.

"Canon Cannon, the bishop's right hand man, has
been murdered."

I remembered Canon Cannon. Canon Shannon Cannon.
A preacher who could sing pretty good baritone but
with a penchant for support groups. He had finally
risen to the top of his profession and was the bishop's
toady. Was. Now, apparently, he was dead as that dead
duck people are always talking about--you know--the
lame one that tried to cross the road.

Tears sprang to Rocki's eyes as she spoke. I wiped
them away with my cigar.

"I know you're busy with that raccoon case, but
here's the thing. Some clerical collars came in the
mail for the bishop," she sniffled. "The bishop didn't
want them so he gave them to Canon Cannon. You know
what a stickler the bishop is. These were size 5 collars with the two-inch reveal. The Bishop's Fashion
Directory states that no bishop should wear anything
less than an 8 1/4 with a two and a half inch reveal.
Anything smaller just looks so pedestrian."

I nodded knowingly. It was the oldest scam in the
book. The old poison-collar trick.

"The bishop wants you immediately. Someone wants
him dead!"

Rocki Pilates leaned across my desk until her

face was close. Very close.

"And I'll be particularly grateful."

I was on the case.

I had never flown business class before, but I liked it. The flight was far from full, and business class was just about empty, so I was surprised to have someone sit next to me. Surprised, but not displeased. She was a real beauty, with black hair and a dark, sultry look set off by a light gray executive business suit. Things could be worse. Just after I had settled in, an attendant was taking my drink order and helping me set my iBook up so I could do a little work. Usually I liked doing my writing on the Underwood, but I thought that the clacking of the keys might be a bit disturbing to the other business class passengers — though I might get by with it in coach. This being a seven-hour flight, I thought I could probably get a couple of chapters finished during the trip. I had coerced Meg into transferring my current efforts onto my laptop before I left.

"I'll do it," she said, "if I don't have to read it."

I was well into my second beer when I heard a throaty "ahem...," followed by, "Are you a writer?" The question came from the seat on my right.

"Why, yes. Yes, I am." I'm sure I was blushing. Wait until Megan heard about this.

"I'm Lindsey Fodor," she said, extending her hand. "I'm a literary agent. Fodor, Sotherman and Marx out of Durham. And since we have quite a few hours together, I wonder if I might read your work?" She smiled and nodded toward the computer. "You never know. Maybe I can give you some pointers. Or sign you to a big contract."

"Any relation to Eugene Fodor?" I asked, smiling back at her. "He was one of my favorite violinists during my college days. I played for one of his master classes once."

"I don't think we're related. He's never shown up at a family reunion or called me with free tickets to a concert. Are you a violinist as well?"

"Accompanist." I scrolled to the top of my manuscript and handed her the computer. She put on her glasses, read for about five minutes and handed the computer back. I looked at her in expectation.

"So," she started, apparently not knowing exactly how to begin her critique. "When you said you were a writer, you meant that you were...?" She paused, her eyebrows up, a question on her face.

"A police detective."

"Thank goodness! And are you as good a detective as you are a writer?"

"Sadly, no. All my talent lies in the writing craft. But, much like Steinbeck, another famous writer, I am unappreciated in my own time." I mustered my best hangdog expression, which was greeted by a laugh.

"Yes, I'm sure you are. You're another Steinbeck, only without the talent. Let me buy you a drink and you can tell me about your brazen use of the nefarious simile." She motioned to the attendant.

"Drinks are free," I said.

"All the better."

The flight over was much more enjoyable than I had anticipated. After supper, another few rounds of drinks and swapping histories, Lindsey fell asleep with her head on my shoulder. I didn't object.

She awoke as the plane was beginning its slow descent and the smell of coffee filled the cabin.

"Just water for me," Lindsey said, and then smiled apologetically to the attendant. "I need to take a pill."

I looked over at the bottle she had put on her tray.

"I used to take that stuff, but they put me on a beta blocker. I was working way too hard and my blood pressure was through the roof."

"Mine is so low, most of the doctors think I'm dead."

The train trip from the Manchester airport into York is two hours of bad scenery. It was already Friday afternoon by the time I cleared customs and would be close to three o'clock when the train pulled in. Lindsey, as it turned out, was traveling to York as well for a writer's conference at the University, so at least I had a traveling companion.

"I'm glad I'm with a seasoned traveler. I never would have found the right train," she said, as we settled into a couple of badly upholstered seats.

"Well, I don't actually know if this is the right one. It doesn't seem to be pointed in the right direction."

I'm always nervous when I first get on a train in another country. There are signs, of course, but they make no sense to Americans. Too much information is taken for granted. For instance, to get to York from Manchester, you have to find the train to Newcastle, which, as every English child knows, makes a stop at York. If you don't know this, however, you're in the soup. You'd think there would be a sign:

THIS IS THE TRAIN TO YORK. GET ON THIS TRAIN.
NO, NOT THAT TRAIN, YOU IDIOT! THAT'S THE TRAIN
TO WICKERSHAM-BADGERTHWAITE-ON-THE-
MARSH FROM WHICH NO ONE EVER RETURNS.
 YOU'LL BE EATEN BY MARSH WOLVES!
But there isn't.

It did happen to be the right train and so, feeling pretty confident as a tour guide and seeing that we had a two-hour trip across the countryside, I took the opportunity to point out the many scenic sheep.

"There's one," I said. Followed shortly by "Look, there's another one."

"OK," Lindsey finally replied with a sigh as we passed through one of the industrial sections of Leeds. "It's not the prettiest train trip I've ever been on, but we're almost there, right?"

"Almost. Another twenty minutes."

"And York is a nice city."

"York is a wonderful city."

York is a city built on Roman and Viking ruins and surrounded by a Roman wall, parts of which date back to the third century. It is a mixture of medieval and modern, — an ancient Roman pillar next to a Starbucks — four-hundred-year-old half-timbered storefronts with windows full of laptop computers and Rolex watches. And at the center and heart of the city is the Minster – the largest gothic cathedral in northern Europe.

After convincing Lindsey that it would be worth her while to hike into town, we came out of the train station and, pulling our suitcases behind us, spotted the huge towers of the cathedral and began our trek. As we walked I did my best impression of a tour guide, telling Lindsey what I knew about the city in general, while at the same time pointing out landmarks with which I was familiar — the River Ouse, the Museum Gardens where the old St. Mary's Abbey stood, Bootham Bar (one of the old Roman gates), and several churches I had explored on earlier visits. Then, finally, after a brisk and somewhat chilly walk, we stood in the shadow of the great church.

After entering the Minster, it took several minutes for our eyes to adjust to the softer light – a gentle radiance that resembled twilight, but gave the stained-glass windows unbelievable clarity. As we walked up the nave toward the choir screen – the architectural division between the nave and the choir containing fifteen life-sized carved images of the early Kings of England – the sound of the pipe organ filled the church. A practice session, presumably, but a lovely and appropriate soundtrack to our tour. We walked around like the rubes we were, our heads tipped backwards, gawking at the grandeur of it all and dragging our American Touristers behind us like a couple of indolent children.

"Where was the murder?" she asked in a whisper as we wandered past yet another monument. I'd given her the bare facts on the plane.

"In the treasury. It's closed though."

"Do you have a camera? Mine's somewhere in my suitcase."

I pulled a small digital camera out of my pocket. "Be prepared," I said. "That's my motto."

"Would you take a picture of me by the kings? My mother would love to see them."

I took some pictures of Lindsey standing in the Minster and promised to e-mail them to her when I returned to the States. We exchanged telephone numbers, e-mail addresses and business cards, and I walked her to a cab heading for the university.

Although I knew I should try to stay awake as long as I could to combat the effects of jet lag, I figured a little nap wouldn't hurt. And besides, if I slept for about an hour, I'd be able to stay awake through Evensong. I walked around the north side of the cathedral, across the small park that nestled into the angles of the great building and through the gate into Minster Yard — a row of houses occupied by the canons of the church. Hugh and his wife Janet lived in one of these houses. Theirs is a rambling, three-story house built about the same time as the cathedral construction was begun. The key was under an old flowerpot in the garden, and before long I was fast asleep, my eyes closing on the vision of the huge stone edifice filling the southwest window.

I awoke to the sound of my travel alarm at half past four. I had time for a quick shower, having figured out the plumbing situation on earlier trips. Plumbing is never to be taken for granted in England. Finishing up quickly, I was in the side door of the Minster, past the policemen's post and sitting in the choir, that area directly behind the screen that divides the nave from the rest of the building, with ten minutes to spare. There were other visitors sitting in adjacent stalls, as was the custom when there was room available.

I settled into the rigid seat of an unnamed Bishop and waited for the service to begin. I gave Hugh a nod as he followed the choir in and took his place with the other clergy. York is so far north that, in February, it's almost dark at five o'clock, making Evensong quite a moving experience, the shadows from the choir's candles bouncing off the fading surfaces at odd angles. On this particular evening the songmen were joined by the girls. A full complement in the Minster Choir consisted of twelve songmen, singing alto, tenor and bass, joined by sixteen girls singing the soprano part. Or, as on this evening, ten songmen and fourteen girls, four of those sniffling. The cold and rainy weather was taking its toll.

On alternate days, the boys sang the soprano parts. I must admit that I'd rather hear the boys, but the girls sang very well, and I'd be around long enough to hear both groups.

We were treated to a *Magnificat* and *Nunc Dimittis,* the evening canticles, set to music by Orlando Gibbons, a Renaissance composer. It was the short service but nevertheless a wonderful treat for the first Friday in Lent. Maybe Megan was right. Maybe I shouldn't torture myself quite so much. The anthem, *Almighty And Everlasting God*, was by Gibbons as well. I closed my eyes and let the sound of the voices wash over me, draining the tension of the journey from my road-weary bones, tension I was unaware of until it was gone.

The choir processed out in silence, the Friday service being unaccompanied by the organ, and I followed them, meeting Hugh outside the sacristy.

"How was your trip?"

"Long. And it gets longer every time, although this was certainly better than last time. If you have a choice, business class is the way to go," I said.

"Only if someone else is paying for it."

"Yep."

"How's Noylene?" he asked. He had heard about her from various e-mails I'd sent, keeping him up to date on St. Germaine happenings, and was intrigued by the lifestyle of the mountain folk.

"Well, she's jes' fahn," I said in my best North Carolina backwoods accent. "She's startin' at the Catawba College of Beauty and Small Engine Repair. We all gits a free haircut and a tune-up once she gits her certifyables."

"Lovely. How about some supper then? I set up your appointment with the Minster Police and the detective from the Police Authority for nine in the morning. Janet is visiting her mother so you can sleep late, but try to be on time for the appointment. They'll probably be civil, but the Police Authority has made it clear that they don't care for Yanks meddling in their cases."

"I'll try to be humble and not mention the American Revolution more than twice."

"Great. Let's eat."

Supper in a pub isn't always a memorable culinary experience. I'm always wary when I see "Spotted Dick" on the menu, but after two days of traveling and a few pints of Guinness, almost anything tastes great. I hit the bed a few hours later and, after musing about Lindsey for a few moments, switched my thoughts over to Megan and slept the sleep of the almost-righteous.

Chapter 3

The next morning found me wide awake at six a.m., which was fine by me. I took a shower, got dressed, and ventured out into the cold February semi-darkness, making my way around the Minster and down Stonegate, before passing the inevitable Starbucks and getting an extra large cup of coffee to go. I could walk the length of the wall – three miles in all – in about an hour and, after wandering through the center of town and dodging the early morning delivery vans, I found one of the many well-worn rock stairwells leading to the top and started off.

An hour later, I had walked off my lethargy and was back at Minster Yard, ready for another cup of coffee and a piece of toast for breakfast. Hugh was up and making the coffee in a French Press – absolutely the most unhealthy and best tasting coffee that there is.

"Have a nice walk?"

"I did, yes."

"Well," Hugh said, "I have some work to do over at the office, but I'll meet you at nine at the treasury."

"OK. I'll be there."

The Minster Treasury is located in the undercroft and can be viewed by anyone with a couple of pounds for admission. After being introduced to Detective Ronald Blake of the North Yorkshire Police Authority and Frank Worthington of the Minster Police, I followed Hugh and the two officers down the steps, and past the Roman ruins unearthed during repairs to the Minster in the late 60's. I walked through the ancient remains, pausing briefly to look at the columns and the Roman well that still survived from the original fortress. Despite the signs advising against it, there were more than a few coins resting on the rocky bottom, courtesy of "well-wishing" tourists. I hadn't ever seen an actual chalk out-line first hand, but there, on the well-worn stones, was a classic rendering. I viewed the scene.

"He was found Monday night after Evensong," Detective Blake said. "Sorry we couldn't leave him here until you could come across. You might have been able to solve the case right away." His sarcasm was evident.

"Hmmm," I said, scratching the back of my neck and trying to look thoughtful. "Maybe I could have. It's hard to say. It's a shame about that revolution, though."

Hugh blanched.

"Huh?" grunted Officer Worthington.

"Well, I'm here now," I said, "and although I'm sure you have the investigation well in hand, for the sake of hands-across-the-sea and all that, maybe you could fill me in."

"Actually, we have no earthly idea why this happened or who did it," said Worthington, trying to avoid the daggers sent his way by the detective's dark look. "This is the most bizarre crime I've ever seen."

"I'll fill you in," said Blake, feigning resignation, "with the facts as we know them. Then you can explain to the family when you get back to the States."

He opened his folder and pulled out a couple of eight by ten photos. The first was an enlargement of a snapshot of a man – slightly built – standing in front of the choir stalls. He had long-ish brown hair, wire-rim glasses, and a fairly long, well-trimmed beard. The second was of the same man, lying sprawled on the floor in the exact position of the chalk outline.

Detective Blake watched me look over the photos, then opened a notebook and began his recitation.

"The victim's name was Kris Toth. He came to York on a Gillette Fellowship and received a position in the Minster Choir.

The choir master and the Dean were glad to have him especially considering the state of the budget and the fact that his fees were paid by the fellowship."

"How did he sing?" I asked.

"Philip says that he was a fairly good baritone," said Hugh. "Not a big voice, but a solid reader."

Blake sniffed impatiently, then continued.

"According to the choir, the victim left the service right after the psalm. That would have been about 5:20. They assumed he was feeling ill. He didn't return and no one saw him again until he was found in the treasury."

"He was found in his choir robe, strangled with a pair of black pantyhose still wrapped around his neck. In his right hand was a cross." Worthington handed me another photo, a close-up of Kris' hand clutching a cross on a chain.

"His prayerbook was there beside him." The detective pointed to the right of the outline.

"Did you check for prints?" I asked.

"We did. The only prints on the cross and the book belonged to the deceased. Another interesting anomaly was the fact that the thumb of his left hand was attached to his fourth finger of the same hand with what has been determined to be a cyanoacrylate adhesive."

"Superglue?" I asked, and Blake shook his head.

"Like Superglue, but with a slightly different chemical makeup. The laboratory is still working on it."

"Did you do an autopsy?" I asked.

"Of course we did an autopsy."

"Wait until you hear this," said Officer Worthington.

"The ambulance took him to the medical center. The medical examiner rang us up about an hour later and called us in. When they removed the choir robe from the victim, they found him dressed in women's underwear. To be more specific, lingerie from Victoria's Secret. Here's a picture."

He handed me another photo, this one showing the body on the examining table. It was the same young man, but no longer in a choir robe. He was wearing a red bustier and red lace panties hooked to open garter belts.

"It's the Valentine's Day Collection," said Worthington, looking over my shoulder.

Blake continued, "The cause of death was strangulation, although he was also hit in the back of the head prior to his death. It is our opinion that the victim was hit first and then strangled."

"Man..."

"That isn't the half of it," said Worthington.

I looked at Detective Blake. He looked back with a cold smile and continued.

"As the autopsy continued, and the underwear came off, another surprising revelation came to light. Kris Toth is, or was, in fact, a woman. Kristina Toth, I presume."

"What? You mean the beard was fake?"

"No, the beard is quite real. The victim apparently suffered from hirsutism, a condition that affects the adrenal gland and causes, among other symptoms, increased hair growth and the thickening of the vocal folds."

"Breasts?"I asked, squinting at the photo.

"Very small. Not uncommon."

"A bearded lady."

"Precisely."

I took some time and looked around the treasury.

"Is anything missing?" I asked.

"No," Worthington said. "We checked the other cabinets.

They were locked and each item still in its place. Everything except the cross."

"What about the one the cross was in?"

"It was locked as well, but the key was in the victim's pocket." He took me over to the cabinet. There, back in its place, was the cross in the photo.

"Do you have video surveillance?"

"Yes, but from sometime after five o'clock when the service started until the service was over, the camera was turned off."

"And no one noticed."

Officer Worthington looked sheepish.

"That was my fault. The officer on duty has a daughter in the choir. They were singing the Stanford service in G and she had the opening solo in the Magnificat. He asked me if it would be permissible for him to go and listen. I told him that he should go."

"Well, that's certainly understandable."

"But not conscionable. The Minster Police have taken their duties seriously for over a hundred and fifty years. When we noticed the camera viewing the treasury was out, we came down and found Kris."

"Was Kris well liked?"

"As far as I could tell. He was a nice enough chap although he kept to himself. Er...herself. She only had one visitor from the states. A cousin, if I remember correctly. Kris introduced her to me."

I looked in the cabinet that housed the pectoral cross. In addition to the cross – a cross that, according to the guidebook I'd picked up, was thought to have been worn by Czar Nicholas II when he was assassinated in 1918 – there was a silver beaker, a wafer bowl – identified as a "ciborium"– and several smaller objects. But as striking as those treasures were, they paled in comparison with the obvious prize. It was a golden chalice – a chalice with a huge diamond mounted in the front. I thumbed through the guidebook and read the description.

Silver gilt chalice made in York, but hallmarked London, 1927.

Attached to the chalice is a 32 carat diamond, the gift of Mrs. Howes, a member of the circus families of Howes and Cushing.

Mrs. Howes was a bareback rider who traveled widely all over America with the circus. She and her husband bought land in various states and made their fortune when the railways were being built in the 19th century.

The diamond and the offer of the chalice in which to set it, were brought unannounced to the Minster by a Miss Forepaugh, one evening in 1927. Miss Forepaugh would only say that Mrs. Howes was an American friend who had recently died, and that she was carrying out her wishes.

No connection between York and the Howes family is known, and there was no reason given for the gift being made to the Minster.

"We've used that chalice in services a time or two," said Hugh.

"It's quite beautiful," I said, looking around the room. "Are you sure nothing's missing?"

"No. We checked all the cabinets. Everything seems to be in order."

"Well, that's it then," I said. "You guys seem to have the investigation well in hand."

"Excuse me?" said Detective Blake.

Hugh looked on in surprise.

"I'll take your report back to the family, although I'm pretty sure they already knew that 'he' was a 'she.'"

"You don't have any insights?" asked Worthington.

"Not really, but I'll think about it and give you a call if I come up with anything."

"Bloody waste of my time," muttered Blake. He snapped his notebook shut and stomped out of the treasury and up the stairs.

I spent the day in York visiting several friends, doing some souvenir shopping, and hearing another Evensong, this time sung by the men and boys. On Sunday morning, Hugh gave me a ride to the train station to catch the 6:25 to the airport.

"Sorry you came all this way for nothing," he said, disappointment still evident in his voice.

"Well, I know you wanted me to solve it right away. I've been studying the question."

The train was pulling up to the platform.

"Tell me something," I said. "The diamond in the chalice. Do you know how it's mounted?"

"Yes, I do. Strangely enough, it's mounted on a silver screw and screwed into the setting."

"Ah," I said, nodding in my most detectorial fashion.

The train had stopped and the doors were opening.

"I think you'll find," I said, putting my suitcase on the train, "that the diamond in the chalice is a fake and has been super-glued into place. The real diamond is gone. Stolen I'd say. Kris Toth was involved somehow and was killed because of it."

Hugh looked stunned.

"Who did it?" he asked.

"I don't know yet. Give me a few weeks. Tell Worthington and have him discover the fake. Then he can announce it to the

Police Authority. It will give the Minster Police some of their credibility back."

"I will."

"Thanks for the trip. Give Janet my best. I'll be in touch."

The doors closed, and the train pulled away from the station.

I got in late on Sunday night and stopped by the church on my way home. Tony's car was still in the parking lot. Father Tony Brown had been the interim priest since Christmas, and things had gone very smoothly subsequent to his return. He had retired the previous summer, but agreed to take back the reins after our new rector, Loraine Ryan, was caught in a few indiscretions. She had been assigned to us by the bishop, something congregations usually buck against, and St. Barnabas was no exception. But now she was gone, and Bishop Douglas had retired as well.

"Hayden," Tony said, smiling, when I rapped on his open door. "How was your trip?"

"It was great. I heard a couple of nice services, did some visiting and worked on a murder investigation."

"Yes, I saw the article in the *Democrat*. It was good."

"Thanks," I said.

"I'm glad you stopped by. I was going to call you tonight anyway. I wanted to tell you that I'm being replaced. There'll be another priest here next Sunday. The acting bishop found someone to take over until we complete our search for a permanent replacement."

"Next Sunday? That fast?"

"He called me yesterday. I announced it to the congregation this morning."

"Ah well, we all knew it was coming. What's the hurry though?" I asked.

"I don't know. This guy is fresh out of seminary. A second

career fellow. He used to be a lawyer."

"Well, he should fit in well here. Still, I think they should have given you a little more notice."

"Ah, it's fine," he said with a big grin. "Maybe they want to give this fellow some experience. I just hope that this time I can stay retired for a couple of months."

Chapter 4

The next morning, she was waiting for me as I came into the office.

"I'm a leper," she said. "And I know there's been a murder."

It was an interesting introduction. My mind wandered back to how it all started. I was walking the streets, streets that exuded a smell that was stale-- stale as day-old flop sweat on a stool pigeon. I had a good nose, a strong Roman nose, a nose that knows, and noses certainly ran in my family - especially when walking the streets. Other families could see trouble. Our family smelled. And I could smell trouble brewing. Or was that Marilyn's coffee?

I had spent the morning picking the hymns for Sunday even though I knew Marilyn would change them. She didn't do it all the time - just enough to make me look bad. Here we were on Transfiguration Sunday and suddenly everyone was singing "It Only Takes A Spark." Subtle, yes, but there were those who knew the difference, and they didn't let me forget a liturgical faux-pas like that.

There was a merger in the works. A merger between two dioceses and it was going to be messy. There were threats on both sides and the bishop wanted me to clear the way for this unholy union. I could do it. I had the goods on every priest in both dioceses. They knew that it was me who filled Mr. Big in on all the ministerial dope. I had the skinny on those birds, and they knew that when this merger took place, any one of them could end up as the priest of the Episcopal

Parish of Weasel Junction.

First on my list was Father Race Rankle, a retired priest from the old mother church with an agenda of his own. The word on the street was that he wanted to use the combined diocesan money to open an Episcopalian leper colony. Father Rankle was leaning heavily toward Biblical precedent, and I knew that if he could get it to a vote, he might just push it through.

Suddenly I was nearly finished with this installment and I realized that there had been no sultry temptress introduced into the plot.

I looked up and there she was--right on cue-- lingering by the stained glass window, dressed in black with a nine foot boa constrictor wrapped around her neck.

"I'm a leper," she said. "And I know there's been a murder."

Somehow I knew she was going to say that.

Meg and I had a huge fire going in the fireplace, doing our best to combat the late snowfall that had covered most of the mountains. I lit a *Romeo et Julietta,* my cigar of choice, surveyed the tranquil domestic scene from my leather club chair, and decided that the setting was the perfect picture of masculine contentment: a huge log cabin with a fire blazing, a beautiful woman reclining in her robe on the couch with a glass of wine in her hand, a loyal dog asleep in front of the fire, a Thelonious Monk CD on the stereo, and an owl sitting on the mounted elk head above the mantle eating a gerbil.

"It's a nice article," said Meg, handing me the paper. "I never knew you were so accomplished."

I looked at last Tuesday's paper. I had been so busy I hadn't had time to read it although I rarely read the paper anyway. The article featured my picture and the facts that I had given to Pete about the murder.

"Pete likes the publicity for the town. It's my civic duty to become famous."

"Tell me how you knew about the diamond," Megan said. "I'm very impressed."

"Elementary, my dear. Here's the skinny."

"The skinny?

"The dope, the poop, the slant, the rap, the hinky."

"Ah, now I understand," she said.

"You see," I began, happy to explain my deductive prowess and show off a little. "You see, Kris Toth, henceforth know as 'the victim' was found dead in the treasury. The first question is 'Why?' She was obviously there to steal something. She also obviously wasn't there by herself."

"The clue there being the fact that she was dead," Meg added.

"Precisely! You know, you're getting the hang of this."

"Please continue."

"The cross was in the victim's hand, so although the case had been opened and re-locked, it appeared that the murderer didn't actually steal anything."

"How odd," said Meg.

"Odd indeed. Now why would the murderer go to all the trouble to murder someone in the treasury with the cameras turned off and not take anything? Especially when a 32 carat diamond worth over a million pounds was there for the taking. The fact that it was screwed into the chalice made it an easy target."

"The superglue gave it away!"

"It was an important clue. You see, the cross was meant to be the only thing the police found missing from the case. They'd assume that the cross had been stolen and never look at the diamond. In the low light of the treasury, a cubic zirconium may not have been discovered for years."

"But how did you know?"

"Given everything else in the case, it was the only thing that made any sense. And I had to ask myself why the victim would have Superglue on her fingers."

"Well, you were right."

I could tell Meg was impressed.

"So who's the murderer?"

"I have a couple of ideas."

"Care to tell?"

"Not yet. I'm still working it out."

"You know," Meg said, looking thoughtful, "if the murderer had put the cross back, you might never have thought to look at the chalice."

"You're right," I said. "That's a very salient point. He might not have had time. Besides, as you know, if the criminal doesn't make at least one mistake, we gum-shoes would be up a dongle."

"Up a dongle?"

"It's detective talk. You know – bounce a limpet, drop a wally, sling some spinach."

"You're making that stuff up."

"Perhaps."

The supper hour came and went, and as I finished up the dishes, Meg finished reading my latest episode.

"Well, your trip to England sure didn't help your writing."

"Oh, I don't know. I think I've tightened it up quite a bit. I met a literary agent, you know. She was quite taken with my prose."

"Yes," Meg said, "I'm sure she was. Is this doggerel going in the choir folders?"

"Yep. This Sunday and every Sunday during Lent."

"That's cruel."

"It may be, but Lent is all about suffering."

"Have you heard anything from Father Tony about the new priest?" Meg asked, changing the subject.

"No, I haven't. I don't know anything about him except that the interim bishop has sent him over from the seminary. To give him some experience, I suppose."

"When will you meet him?"

"He'll be here on Wednesday to talk to everyone. I guess he knows he's just a sub until we finish the search for our new guy."

"What about the new Christian education director? What's her name? Brandi? Boopsie? Have you talked with her?"

"Yes, I have," I answered. "Her name's Brenda, and I'm reserving judgment. So far she's been kind of quiet during staff meetings, but I get the feeling she's just biding her time. She mentioned that at her last church they had a 'Flower Communion' and that it was a very meaningful service. Everyone brought a flower and put it on the altar. During the sermon, the members of the congregation were invited to stand and say a few words about their particular flower."

"You can't say anything bad about her, you know. Not after you got Loraine fired."

"I did not get Loraine fired," I said, my hackles rising involuntarily. "She got herself fired."

"Nevertheless," said Meg, "you'd better lay low for a while."

"You have my promise. I won't say anything to anyone until we actually get a full-time priest. I'll just go with the flow, direct the music, plant some flowers, and let the chips fall where they may."

"That's a good plan," said Meg.

The mood at the Slab was upbeat although the crowd was small. The economy of St. Germaine relies mainly on tourism, most of the visitors arriving during the four to six weeks of leaf season – October and early November. We get a few die-hards on long weekends during snow season, but we don't have any slopes, so the skiers tend to stay up on Sugarloaf or somewhere closer to the action. In the summer, we get some folks intent on escaping the heat of the lowlands. Late February, on the other hand, with its bitter wind, ice, frequent snows, and overcast days doesn't draw the tourists like the mayor of St. Germaine thought it should.

"Where are all the customers?" asked Pete of no one in particular.

"Pete," I said, "as mayor of this burg, it is your duty to go out and round up some tourists."

Pete looked thoughtful. "The article in the paper about you and the York investigation was pretty good. It went statewide, you know. I pulled a few strings." He stared out the window for a moment. "Maybe the weather has something to do with it."

"Do you really think so?" asked Nancy. She was eating her regular breakfast of flapjacks and coffee. "The temperature's already up to ten degrees. I'll bet they come flocking in for the crowning of the Ice Princess."

Dave came in the door, pulling it closed against the wind.

"Now that we're all here," I said, "we can call this meeting of the St. Germaine Police Force and Tourism Review Board to order."

"I move that we all go to Barbados," said Nancy.

"What? And give up all this?" Dave was stomping the snow off his boots and taking off his coat.

It was my turn. "I don't know about you folks, but I love this weather. Think about it. No crime – too cold. No waiting for a table – too cold. No traffic – too cold."

"No customers," said Pete. "No tourists. No business. No rent. No money."

"Trust you to always find the down side. You always were a pessimist. My cup, on the other hand, is half full." I held my coffee cup aloft, motioning to Noylene for a refill.

"Mine is half empty," admitted Pete, holding his cup up as well.

"Mine's half frozen," said Noylene, filling both cups, "and you people are crazy."

The staff meeting at St. Barnabas on Wednesday morning was well attended and what I would describe as rather eventful. Our new interim priest was in attendance, presumably to meet us all and to be introduced by Father Tony. Decorum, in these circumstances, calls for a humble, self-effacing response to this presentation. We all probably expected it, but it was not to be.

Father Emil Barna was a short, unattractive man with a bad toupee in a suspicious auburn color. He was, according to his recitation, a "second career" priest, his first career being an ambulance-chasing attorney of some note in Durham. He had now found the higher calling. As a "very wealthy individual," he was now ready to begin his ministry without thought to his compensation, although he had decided, after much prayer, that it was in the church's best interest for him to accept the salary.

I pointed out that as a "very wealthy individual" myself, I gave my own salary back to the church. He looked as if he didn't hear me and continued.

"I think you'll find that, although I'm not an easy person to work for, I'm inevitably right in my decisions. If all of you will pull together as a ministry team and follow the few simple rules that I have, everything will run very smoothly."

"Now I've already spoken with Brenda Marshall. Since she's in charge of Christian education..." He looked to Brenda, and she smiled and nodded like the cat that had just eaten the science fair project. "We have agreed that she should take charge of our worship planning as well as our Sunday School and Wednesday night Institute programming. I think we're all on the same page here."

I snorted into my coffee, but didn't say anything. Father Tony had turned a wonderful shade of pale.

"Brenda," I asked, rather innocently I thought, "didn't you come to us from a Presbyterian congregation?"

"Yes, but my background will add diversity to our offerings." She looked around the table confidently. True to my promise to Meg, I smiled and nodded.

"I'm sure it will."

Father Barna cleared his throat in such an obvious manner that all attention turned back to him. He tapped on his yellow notepad with his pen.

"Hayden Konig," he said, reading off the paper. "Did I pronounce that correctly?"

I nodded with a smile.

"Hayden, you will direct the choir and play for the services. I'll want to pick the hymns in consultation with Ms. Marshall. I think she and I have a good feel for what the people will like."

"That's just fine," I said. Father Tony was stock still, the only evidence of his burgeoning anger manifesting itself in his reddening nostrils and bloodless knuckles.

The Reverend Barna continued.

"This will be Father Brown's last Sunday, so I will begin on Monday morning. I expect you all to be here bright and early for an eight o'clock staff meeting."

"Sorry, Emil," I said. "I'm also the chief of police, and I have a meeting first thing on Monday. I'll tell you what. Since Brenda's

45

in charge of the services, why doesn't she just put a list of the hymns and the service music on the organ, and I'll look through it on Wednesday night before choir practice. I presume you'd still like me to pick the anthems for the choir."

"Of course," he said with a dismissive wave of his hand.

"I'll give the titles to Brenda for the bulletin."

"Yes, yes. That's fine. Whatever," he said, and then continued.

"Now, I'm going to be making a few changes around here. The first is that we're going to add a little pomp to the services. I will be processing along with the choir, the thurifer and the acolytes. However, I'm going to need a verger and two more attendants to carry the back of my cope in procession. Hayden, can you take care of that?"

"No, I don't think so."

He looked rather startled.

"You," he said, pointing at Beverly Greene, one of the two Altar Guild representatives. "What's your name?"

"Beverly...um...Greene," she answered hesitantly.

"Yes, Ms. Greene," he said, taking particular care to pronounce 'mizz' in a politically correct fashion – extra emphasis on the 'zz'. "Will you take care of getting those attendants for me?"

"Er...yes, I guess so."

"Good. That's done then. I have a verger that's coming with me. He's my valet and a top-notch verger. I'll speak to the vestry about getting him appointed and on the staff. That's all then. You're dismissed. Brenda, come with me." He looked around the table. "I'll see *most* of you on Monday morning."

He picked up his pad and was out the door, followed closely by Brenda Marshall, before I could even start laughing. Which I did – at length – as soon as the door closed.

"Oh man," said Elaine, the other Altar Guild representative.

"We are in for it."

Father Tony was so mad he couldn't even get a word out.

"Meg says that I have to play nice," I explained to the remaining attendees of the introductory meeting, "which is why I didn't even mention the ground-hog pelt sitting atop his head."

"I hear he has a wife," Beverly said.

"And that she's even worse," Elaine chimed in.

"How is the Priest Selection Committee coming with the resumés?" I asked.

"Well, they didn't meet last week," said Tony. "But I'll get them back together tonight. And at least once more before I leave."

Chapter 5

"That's funny, you don't look like a leper."

I must admit that it wasn't the best pick-up line I've ever used. Sometimes I went with "What's your sign?", sometimes with "Don't I know you from someplace?" This was a new one. But if it worked, I'd keep it in the repertoire.

She stood by the window, the sun racing across her snake-stained dress, looking like ... well ... a very good-looking leper. I lit a cigar.

"You should really have that dress cleaned," I puffed, the smoke coming out of my mouth like the exhaust from a Yugo with a bad ring job. "Those snake stains are pretty disgusting."

"Silly boy. Don't you know that a leper can't change her spots?" She giggled. One of her ears fell off and landed on my desk. She quickly put it into her pocketbook and returned to the reclining position by the window. I knew she was hoping I didn't see her little gaffe because it's hard to seduce someone when your facade is coming apart.

She laughed again, this time nervously. "I just can't seem to keep those dried apricots in my hair."

"Listen sister," I growled. "I haven't got time for this. What's your game?"

I knew about her, of course. Lilith Hammerschmidt, the leprous and distant relation to Andreas Hammerschmidt, the early baroque composer of some note, and a fine musician in her own right. Or so I had heard. I had also heard that the specific kind of leprosy with which she was infected was relatively non-contagious. At least the snake looked healthy--and hungry. I took a hamster out of my pocket and threw it into the middle of the floor, and he was on it like Doberman frosting on a poodle cake.

"Do you always keep hamsters in your pants?"

I changed the subject. I was good at this game and she knew it. I lit another cigar.

"What's the deal, Lilith? Is the bishop setting me up again?"

"I don't know anything about it. All I know is that we've got to have the leper Colony approved. I'm here on behalf of the Crofton Chamber of Commerce. I'm their official lobbyist." She pulled off her glove and put her thumb back in her purse.

Suddenly and without warning, I heard a startling sound. It was not unlike the great bass, Hans Hotter, singing the entire score to "Die Winterreise" by Franz Schubert, but in a much lower key. I looked around the room. It was a deep, deep sound and resonant. It was a sound I had been looking for to complete my choir, and it seemed to be coming from the snake.

"Is that the hamster, or is the snake singing German lieder?"

She smiled and two teeth dropped to the carpet, lying there like a couple of yellow Chicklets. "It's just Rolf. He's highly musical."

"Aaaargh!" said Meg, doing her best pirate impression and slamming the kitchen door. She had picked up "Aaaargh!" from me, I suppose, it being one of my favorite buccaneer expressions. I like to think I'm a good influence.

"I don't know if I can take this priest, even as an interim."

"He is singularly unlikable."

"I was 'informed' that I was required at the worship meeting this morning."

"And how did that go?"

"All I can say is 'Aaaargh!'"

"Well put."

"You," she said, with a sudden gleam in her eyes. "You can do something."

"No, I can't. Remember my Lenten resolve. I shan't make any trouble for the man. Or his toady, Brenda, either. I am the model of a good employee."

"She's a piece of work," Meg said. "And guess what? His valet has arrived. We haven't met him yet, but the plan is to install him as verger, then have the vestry hire him and put him on staff."

"I had heard that."

"So, what's a verger for Pete's sake? And why do we need one? And if we did need one, why would we hire the priest's valet? And why does a priest *need* a valet?"

"All very good questions."

"Well?"

"Hmmm," I started. "A verger is basically the person who marshals the procession, but they're usually associated with cathedrals. They have a very nice stick and they point where everyone in the procession should go. I suppose they can have other duties as well, sort of like ushers. As far as St. Barnabas is concerned, I think that a verger would be just hilarious. I'm for it."

"As to why our new priest needs a valet, perhaps it's to keep that ferocious toupee from escaping and making a meal out of someone's house-cat."

"You're not being serious here."

"Oh yes I am. It's Lent, remember?"

"Here's the other thing. Princess Foo-Foo has decided to

institute a Children's Moment in the service right before the office hymn."

"Princess Foo-Foo?"

"Brenda. You know. Our director of Christian ed. She's very 'feeling-oriented.'"

"I didn't know she knew what an office hymn was. But now that I think about it, yes. Yes, a Children's Moment should be fun," I said. "It will allow the children to be the center of attention as well as terrifying the parents and entertaining the congregation to no end. It's win-win all around and just plain good church."

"We went through this before. Remember?"

"I do remember."

"And you were against it."

"Yes, but now I'm for it," I replied with a smile.

"Aaaargh!"

As Children's Moments go, I thought the first one by our new interim priest went rather well. We hadn't met the priest's valet, and the office of verger hadn't been sanctioned, so we were still vergerless. We did have two extra acolytes to carry the tails of the priest's cope. They were instructed to keep the cope off the ground at all times – something not that easy to accomplish given the fact that the cope was easily a foot too long for the priest. Still, the acolytes scurried around behind him wherever he went like a couple of hyperactive bridesmaids trying to keep the bridal train straight for the photographer. The choir was horrified and kept glancing my way, perhaps thinking that I would finally put the Beretta 9mm I kept under the organ bench to good use. I, however, looked on with an expression I hoped might be described as "expectant wonder."

After the second hymn, Father Barna announced that the

children should come forward to spend a few quality moments with their spiritual leader. Four children came forward. The rest clung to their parents like infant chimpanzees, their faces hidden in fear of being forced to participate.

"Good morning," said the priest in his best child-friendly voice, a voice I presume he'd been practicing all morning. "I'm Father Barna. Today I'd like to tell you a Bible story."

"What's that on your head?" asked Moosey loudly. Moosey McCollough was a particular favorite of mine. His father had named the three McCollough children after various beers before he abruptly disappeared, leaving their mother, Ardine, with the trailer, the kids, and no money to speak of. Bud, the oldest, was fourteen. Pauli-Girl was twelve. Little Moose-Head, Moosey for short, was six and the most gregarious of the clan.

Father Barna pretended he hadn't heard the question and started again.

"Today I'd like to tell you a Bible story."

"Is this one about a dinosaur?" asked Bernadette. Bernadette was five and a half.

"No, it's not about a dinosaur," said Father Barna.

"Is this the story about the ark and the rainbow and the dove and the animals, two-by-two?" asked Ashley. "Because if it is, we already know that one." Ashley was Bernadette's best friend. The other boy was Robert, a precocious kindergartener. Together – Moosey, Bernadette, Ashley and Robert were the Fearsome Foursome of the Sunday School and every teacher's nightmare.

"No," said the priest, answering Ashley's question. "It's not about the ark."

"Is it the story about David and the giant and the five smooth stones?" asked Robert.

The questions were coming fast now.

"No," said Father Barna, sweat starting to form under the

edges of his hairpiece, causing the ends to curl ominously.

Robert: "Is this the story..."

"No! Now just listen. This is the story of Gideon and his fleece."

It was Moosey's turn. "Gideon and his fleas?"

"Yes. Once upon a time, before Jesus was born, there was a King named Gideon."

Bernadette was next. "Was he an evil king?"

"No. He was a good king. God told Gideon to attack the army that was threatening the Israelites."

Ashley: "I would do it. I'd sure do it if God said so. God's sort of like your father – only bigger."

They were tag-teaming now. A well-oiled, unrehearsed juggernaught. Father Barna was beginning to squirm.

"Of course you'd do it. But Gideon was afraid and didn't want to attack."

Moosey: "He was probably just all itchy."

"Itchy?" said Father Barna. "Why?"

"Because of his fleas."

Father Barna did his best to ignore the comment, obviously confused, much to the congregation's delight. This was, as they say in show biz, what they had paid to see.

"Well, I suppose," said the priest trying to get back on track. "Anyway, Gideon told God that he would put his fleece on the ground and if it was wet in the morning when the ground was dry, he would know God would help him win."

Moosey: "So he put his fleas on the ground?"

"Yes."

"And were they wet?"

"Yes," said Father Barna.

"And then did he take them back?" Moosey was pushing him for answers.

"Well, I suppose he did."

Moosey thought hard for a moment. The church became very still as everyone waited expectantly for his next observation. Even the other children demurred to his next theological revelation.

"When our dog scratches," Moosey said thoughtfully, "we have to put some powder on him. He doesn't like it much."

This caught Father Barna by surprise. "Huh? No. No, I suppose he doesn't."

"Who won the battle?" asked Bernadette, pulling her dress up over her head, peeking out just in time to see her mother cover her face with her hands in abject horror.

"Gideon's army won," said Father Barna, "but the story isn't..."

"Did the whole army have fleas?" asked Moosey.

"No, just Gideon I think, but..."

Moosey interrupted. "Mom says that we could all get them because they get in the carpet and lay eggs."

"What?" Father Barna croaked, now close to panic.

"Can I pet your head?" asked Robert.

"Our last priest gave us candy," said Ashley, pulling on his robe and trying to get into his pockets.

"This is my favorite dress," said Bernadette, raising and lowering her skirt to show off her new Barney underpants. "But Momma says it's a bitch to iron."

Chapter 6

"How much for the snake?" I wanted that snake. It would cinch my victory at the Bishop's Invitational Choral Tournament. I was just one voice away, and this could be it.

She picked Rolf up carefully so as not to squeeze the still-wriggling, tennis-ball sized lump that was about eight inches down his throat.

"He only sings when he's fed."

I had plenty of hamsters and I knew how to use them.

"How much?" I asked again, eyeing the reptile with greedy eyes.

Suddenly I looked up. There was a gun in her hand that gave me a bad case of barrel envy. A gun in one hand and a nine-foot boa constrictor in the other. Somebody was going to get it, and I was afraid it was going to be me.

"Marilyn," I called, "How about a cup of coffee?"

"You know I love you. Right, honey?" asked Meg.
"Yes."
"This is really bad."

"Hayden! You aren't going to believe this!"

Beverly and Elaine had both come into the police station and were hollering across the counter. Dave had gone out for donuts, or he might have been able to restore a little decorum.

"Come on in. Quit yelling," I called from my desk.

They came around the counter and through the door of my cluttered office. I turned down the stereo and listened to both of them launch into a tirade-duet.

"One at a time," I said. "Tell me what's going on."

"It's the valet!" said Elaine.

"He's a dwarf!" shouted Beverly.

"I believe they like to be called 'little people'," I said. "But why do you think he's a dwarf? Maybe he's just short."

"He TOLD us that he was a dwarf!" Elaine said. "I just can't believe this."

"I couldn't even understand him," said Beverly. "He's Hungarian! And he doesn't speak English all that well."

I nodded. "So, he's a Hungarian dwarf. And his name is...?"

"I wrote it down. Hang on," said Beverly, digging a piece of paper out of her purse. "Here it is. His name is Wenceslas. Wenceslas Kaszas. He's royalty or something."

I could tell I was smiling in spite of myself. I had heard about the priest's valet. Word travels fast around St. Germaine, and having a Hungarian dwarf in town was a tough secret to keep.

"I don't think that Wenceslas is a Hungarian name. It's more Czech I think. Good King Wenceslas and all that."

"It doesn't matter," said Elaine, despair evident in her voice. "Our verger is a Hungarian dwarf. What are we going to do?"

"I guess we'll make do until we get our new priest."

"Can't you do something, Hayden?"

"Nope. Sorry. We just have to wait it out."

As I watched Elaine and Beverly cross the street and head straight for the library, presumably to spread the news to whomever they could find, Dave came in the front door with the donuts.

"What's going on?" he asked. He put the box of donuts on the counter, opened it and took two of them back to his desk.

"Nothing earthshaking. Just a little Episcopal Church politics."

"Oh, you mean the dwarf. They were talking about him down at Dizzy Donuts."

"Really? They were talking about it? I thought Dizzy D's was a Methodist hangout."

"I don't know about that," Dave said, "but St. Barnabas should be full next Sunday. Everyone will be there. It's all they're talking about." Dave took a big bite of his breakfast.

"Answer the phone please, Dave," I said in response to the insistent ringing and my eagerness to cut this conversation short.

"Mmmph," said Dave through a mouthful of banana crème filling.

"Never mind," I said. "I'll get it."

Hugh was on the phone. I mentally figured the time difference. It was mid-afternoon in England.

"How's the new priest?" he asked.

"Um. Well, he's certainly eminently unqualified, yet at the same time, highly amusing."

"Great," he said, changing the subject. "Do you have any more thoughts on the murder?"

"Yes I do. I believe I've solved the entire crime, but I'll have to have another trip over to explain everything to the Police Authority. Did you check out the diamond?"

"Yes, we did. It was a fake, just as you said, and the real diamond is still missing. Any ideas where it might be?"

"Yep."

"Well?"

"If I tell you now, it won't be a surprise."

I could hear a heavy sigh on the other end of the phone.

"Ok, ok," I said. "I don't actually know yet. It would be easier if I had about a week over there to question a few folks and look around again."

"I'll see what I can arrange. Your stock is pretty high since your discovery of the fake diamond. The Minster Police are holding up their heads again."

"Let me know when. Things are pretty slow here."

Nancy came in a few minutes later, grabbed a couple of donuts, and sat down at her desk.

"I heard about your dwarf," she said.

"First of all, he's not *my* dwarf. He's the priest's dwarf ...er...valet."

"The priest has a valet?"

"Well," I started, hating to be put in the position of defending this nitwit, "maybe the valet is left over from his lawyerin' days. All lawyers need a valet. At least that's what I've heard."

"I'm going to become a lawyer," said Dave. "I need a valet."

"Yeah, Dave," said Nancy, reaching for the phone, now ringing again. "You need someone to lay out your khakis and keep track of your dates." She lifted the phone to her ear.

"Police Department. Uh huh. Just a second. I'll get him." She pointed to me and pushed half a donut into her mouth.

"Hayden Konig," I said.

"Hayden, this is Malcolm."

This was the call I'd been dreading all morning.

"Hi, Malcolm. What's new?"

"You know exactly what's new."

Malcolm Walker was the Senior Warden of St. Barnabas. He was in charge of the vestry, the church finances, and was the richest man in St. Germaine. He was currently separated from his second wife, Rhiza, whom I knew quite well from graduate school. Rhiza had moved to Blowing Rock just after Christmas, and I saw her occasionally. We were still great friends. Malcolm and I were less friendly, but in spite of our past differences, still on good terms.

"Listen, Malcolm. I'm staying out of all of this. The bishop assigned this guy for reasons unknown to anyone with any sense, but I'm going to ride it out."

"He wants the vestry to hire his valet to be the verger."

"I'd heard that."

"Look, Hayden," he said. "Everyone respects your opinion. Apparently you're now the only person employed by the church that has any sense of liturgy at all. Might I convince you to speak out on this subject?"

"I don't think I can, Malcolm. The priest is the boss until he's no longer the priest. So, until the bishop replaces him, which doesn't seem likely, it's up to the vestry to do the best they can. Admittedly, that probably won't be too much. You can refuse to hire the verger, but I think Emil will use him anyway."

"I suppose. I've already left several messages with the bishop, but he hasn't returned my calls."

"On the up-side, the word is that St. Barnabas should be full on Sunday."

"Oh, that's just great." Malcolm sighed into the phone. "I'll talk to you later," he said and hung up.

Nancy had already picked up another call on line two. "It's for you," she called. "It's Connie Ray."

"Hi, Connie. What's up? Yeah. Yeah. Hmmm. I don't know what we can do, but I'll ask around. Someone might know something. No, don't shoot anybody. I'll talk to you later."

Nancy looked at me waiting for the news.

"That was Connie Ray."

"Yeah, I know."

"He's been having some problems out at the farm."

Nancy nodded.

"I'm afraid it's..." I paused for dramatic effect, my eyes narrowing, "cow tipping."

"It's too cold for cow tipping," Dave chimed in. "That's a summer sport."

"These are in the barn. It's cold, sure, but at least there's a lot of hay around."

Pete Moss stuck his head in the door.

"If any of you want a haircut," he announced, "I'm offering a free trim with any sandwich combo plate. Noylene has just graduated from Beauty College."

"We'll be there shortly," I said. "I always like to support our local artists."

"What about the cow tipping?" Nancy asked as Pete continued down the street, making his luncheon announcement to the various businesses remaining open through the cold winter months. She had her pad out and was getting ready to take notes.

"Last time, it was those high school kids from Watauga South," Dave said.

"Probably more of the same," I said. "Let's stop it though before some poor cow gets hurt. Who's up for barn duty? Nancy?"

"Ah, crime fighting in the big city." Nancy was resigning herself to spending the night in a cold barn. "I'm taking Dave with me," she said.

"Fine with me," I answered, knowing that Dave would love it. An evening alone in a dark barn with Officer Parsky. What could be better? I think the Rubaiyat said it best.

A book of verses underneath the boughs;
A loaf of bread, a jug of wine, and cows.

Lenten Cow Tipping. What next?

Chapter 7

Someone was in trouble and it was probably me. We detectives can sense these things almost instinctively, that and the fact that there was a forty-five pointed straight at my head by a woman wearing black, picking body parts off my carpet like a crusader finding relics in the Holy Land, and holding a nine foot boa constrictor named Rolf.

"You're coming with me," said Lilith, waving her piece around like Toscanini at a Mahler festival.

"Where are we going?" I asked.

"The circus."

Brahms' First Symphony was heading into the slow movement just as the pork chops were nearing culinary perfection.

"I don't keep up with the latest trends," said Megan as I finished telling her about our newest police case. "What the heck is cow tipping?"

She moved around the table, setting the plates and silver with uncommon ease considering she had to maneuver her way over and around a sprawling dog that had made himself comfortable in the middle of the kitchen floor.

"It's sort of a prank, but it's been around for years. High school kids do it for fun, especially in rural areas."

"Well, we certainly qualify in that regard."

"You sneak up on a sleeping cow, give it a firm but hard push, and the cow will fall right over."

"And you know this because...?"

"We were all young once." I opened a beer and took a long pull from the bottle.

"I thought you had given up beer for Lent," Meg said.

"I started to, but then I decided to give up meddling in church politics. In order to do that, I'm going to need the beer."

"OK then. Back to the cows."

"Anyway," I continued, "when the cow falls over, it tends to give a startled moo, which in turn wakes up all the other cows. If there happens to be a bull around, you'd better be fast. The problem is that sometimes the cows injure themselves in the fall. These are very expensive animals, especially some of Connie's milk cows. They're worth several thousand dollars apiece."

"The whole thing is just silly."

"I know it. Anyway, Connie Ray's getting a donkey."

"A watch donkey?"

"Exactly. They tend to sound an alarm and wake the cows up before they can be tipped. And they're good protection against coyotes."

"We don't have any coyotes around here, do we?" Meg asked.

"I haven't seen any, but that doesn't mean they aren't out there lurking."

"Not to change the subject, but that's an interesting haircut you have there."

"It was free with the Reuben combo plate at the Slab. Noylene Fabergé graduated from Beauty School yesterday. She was giving haircuts in the back of Pete's storeroom."

"If I were you, I'd rethink the 'free haircut with lunch' scenario. At least it's winter. You can wear a hat until it grows out."

"It's not that bad, is it?"

"No. Not that bad. But I'd give Noylene a couple of months practice before I became a regular."

"I'll take that advice."

Sunday morning at St. Barnabas was as well attended as it was advertised to be with Wenceslas making his debut as verger to great acclaim. I played quite a prelude – The Bach d-minor with the fugue following. Trite, perhaps, but with a royal Hungarian dwarf leading the procession, I couldn't think of anything more appropriate.

The procession began with the verger, dressed elegantly in a black velvet tunic, complete with a velvet tam and an ostrich plume. His kept his wand at a precise forty-five degree angle, the silver tip pointing the way, and stepped out like he had been trained in the Hungarian Red Army. His boots were polished to a dazzling shine and his cape was trimmed in dark fur. He had a manicured, white beard and a large handlebar moustache. I had to admit that he looked every bit of the Hungarian royalty that we had heard he was. All eyes were on him as he executed a kick turn in front of the altar, spun the verge in his hand like a drum major, and pointed each member of the procession to his place – all in rhythmic precision. As the thurifer brought the incense pot up to the altar, Wenceslas seemed to disappear into the cloud of smoke, reappearing in his designated place as if by magic. I could see all this out of the corner of my eye, and I could see the choir as well. They were mesmerized.

The priest was less impressive in his entrance. He still had his attendants scurrying around behind him, trying to keep his cope off the ground. However, where Wenceslas had an air of dignity and purpose, the priest had none.

The Children's Moment had been mercifully scrapped, so the rest of the service went pretty much without incident. It was the following morning that the next bombshell hit.

"Nice of you to come to our staff meeting, Hayden," said Father Barna in what I perceived as a rather sarcastic tone.

"It's my pleasure to be here, Emil," I said, taking a sip of coffee.

"I'm sure we'd all like to welcome the newest member of my staff," Father Barna continued. "This is my excellent valet and our new verger, Wenceslas Kaszas."

Wenceslas nodded and surveyed the table before addressing us in his thick Hungarian accent.

"For those of you that are wondering," he said carefully, "I am a dwarf. I am not a little person. I am from Budapest where I was the verger for Archbishop Erdo."

"Roman Catholic?" I asked.

"Of course."

Wenceslas had a thick Hungarian accent. I felt like I was talking to Bela Lugosi.

"You're an excellent verger," I said. "Way too accomplished for a small church like St. Barnabas." It was not empty praise. He was way out of our league.

He nodded at me. "Yes, but I do not think I will be here for a long time."

"Isn't 'Wenceslas' a Czech name?" I asked.

"Yes," he nodded again, his mustache bobbing slightly. "But I was named for Wenceslas Három, the old King of Hungary."

"Enough chit-chat," said Father Barna. "It's very important to get to my agenda. First on the list – the Children's Moment. I don't think it worked terribly well. I think we should suspend it until after Easter."

There were nods all around the table. I tried not to grin.

"Next, we have a report from Brenda."

Princess Foo-Foo started flipping through her papers until she found the one she needed.

"I've decided," she started. "That is, Father Barna and I have decided..." She smiled across the table at him. "...that Lent would be a good time to have our first Clown Eucharist."

"Our what?" said Georgia Wester, obviously appalled. Georgia was a LEM, that is, a Lay Eucharistic Minister, and she took her job seriously.

"Lent is such a gloomy season. It would be a good time to lighten things up a little. I think this would be a fabulous opportunity for everyone in the congregation to find their happy place."

"I agree," said Father Barna, not wanting to appear too far away from the action. "It's going to be our theme for the next few weeks. We'll discuss it in the Sunday School classes and offer workshops during Institute on Wednesday evenings. Brenda has found us a workbook book called *Finding Your Inner Clown*. We've ordered fifty books and I'd like two volunteers to facilitate the classes. Brenda? You'll be there of course."

The Princess nodded.

"Hayden, can you be there as well?"

"I'd like to, but I have that class on comparative religions to 'facilitate,'" I said, thinking quickly.

"I didn't know about that. Was it on the schedule?"

"I'm pretty sure it was," I said, trying to catch Marilyn's eye. She was dutifully taking notes as any good secretary should.

"Here it is," said Marilyn, looking up and flipping a couple pages for show, never missing a beat. "I'm sorry. I hadn't put it on the calendar yet."

I mentally put Marilyn down for a nice birthday gift.

"Then I suppose Brenda will have to do it herself," said Father Barna. "We'll culminate the class with the Clown Eucharist on Sunday morning. That's the Sunday after next."

"I hesitate to ask," I said. "But what the heck is a Clown Eucharist?"

"We'll have a couple of professional clowns come in," Princess Foo-Foo said. "Father Barna will dress up as a clown and we'll ask for some parishioners to get involved as well. We'll also need some mimes and dancers. Everyone involved will dress as a clown to uphold the feeling of clown-ness."

"Wenceslas?" I asked. I couldn't see him donning a clown suit.

"Alas, I will not be here that week."

"Alas," I said.

"I owe you one," I said to Marilyn as I walked by her desk on the way out.

"You sure do. But you're not out of trouble yet. You still have to get a class together on comparative religions. Father Barna wants me to put it in the newsletter."

"It's OK," I said. "I have a couple of ideas. I'll call a few of my other-denominational friends and have them come and chat with whoever shows up. Who knows? It might even be fun."

"No good deed goes unpunished, you know," she said.

I was trying to get into the office fairly early the next morning. The sun was up, but hadn't yet made its way over the mountain when I got into my 1962 pick-up, put on Britten's *War Requiem* and pulled onto the main road. The *War Requiem* is a dark, complex piece and suited my mood as well as the weather. Thirty days of below freezing temperatures took its toll on even the most ardent proponents of an extended winter, myself included.

Nancy had beaten me to the office and was checking the answering machine as I came in.

"Anything good?"

"Nope," she said. "A barking dog at three a.m. I actually got the call last night, but it was too cold to mess with."

"I agree. Are you going to the barn on Friday?"

"I have my long-johns ready."

"I won't be here. I'm off to Atlanta on Friday morning for a couple of days," I said. "There's a conference I'm supposed to attend. I'll be back on Saturday night."

"Hmmm," Nancy said. "You get to go to Atlanta. I get to sit in a barn in the freezing cold all night with 'Dave the Wonder Cop' waiting for cow-tippers. Yet, strangely, you make more money than me."

"Yes, but you have a bigger gun. The ways of law enforcement are weird and wonderful. Let's get over to The Slab and get some coffee. It's colder than a witch's nose in here."

"A witch's nose? Don't you mean a witch's ti..."

"Ah, ah," I said, interrupting her. "That could be construed as harassment."

"And me with a bigger gun."

Meg met me for an early lunch at a new establishment that had opened downtown. The Ginger Cat was what I would describe as an upscale chowder bar catering to a wealthy and touristy clientele. In the rear of the store there was a small eatery featuring various soups and homemade breads, coupled with a shop in the front featuring local and regional arts and crafts. As I walked in, I noticed one of Ardine McCollough's quilts sporting a hefty price tag of four hundred fifty dollars.

"Morning, Hayden," said Annie. Annie Cooke lived in Boone but had opened The Ginger Cat in St. Germaine to take advantage of the slightly longer tourist season.

"Good morning, Annie. How's business?"

"Awful. I had to let one girl go last week. I told her to try back in the spring, but she'll probably find other work by then. You know my other girl, Cynthia Johnsson. She just wanted part-time work anyway, so I gave her a few weeks off. I guess it's this way for everyone this time of year."

"I'm afraid so," I said. "No crime though. That's a plus."

"For you maybe. I'll bet an interesting crime or two would help perk up business."

"Is Megan here yet?"

"Just came in." She nodded toward the tables in the back. "Mind the crowds," she added with more than a hint of sarcasm.

I made my way to the back and joined Meg at a table for two.

"We're probably going to be the only customers," she said, "so we have our choice of soup – French Onion or French Onion with bacon sprinkles."

"No kidding? Sprinkles? I'll have that."

"It's on the stove even as we chat. Care for a muffin?"

"Yes, please," I said, lifting one from the basket, taking care to keep my pinkie aloft in my most genteel manner.

"I hear you're doing a class on comparative religion for Wednesday night Institute. I can't decide whether to take your class or 'Finding Your Inner Clown' from Princess Foo-Foo."

"Wow. Word travels fast."

"So, the question I have for you is," she continued, ignoring my interruption, "why should I come to your class instead of searching diligently for my happy place?"

"Well, we're the only ones here. How 'bout if I show you where your happy place is right now?" I said, raising a rakish eyebrow.

"Stop that this minute. This is a civilized and proper luncheon."

"Well, I don't know which will be more entertaining," I said, taking a delicate nibble of my muffin. "But I called a couple of guest lecturers. This Wednesday we will be hosting Mr. Julian Mayberry from the Raelians followed by Brother Harley Ray Hammond from the Apostolic Four-Square Pentecostal Holiness Temple of God with Signs Following."

"Really? The Raelians? That sounds like much more fun than

finding a clown, even an inner one. I do like a good circus though."

"I'm afraid that's what you're going to get."

We met Karen Dougherty at the door of the Ginger Cat just as we were leaving. Karen was the St. Germaine doctor, semi-retired, with a full-time schedule.

"Hayden," she said with a smile. "Just the person I want to see!"

"I suggest the soup with sprinkles," I said, always happy to offer my culinary suggestions.

"Hi Meg. Soup with sprinkles? Is that on the menu?"

"Ignore him," Meg said. "He's full of himself today."

"I wanted to talk to you anyway," said Karen. "I'm heading up a school program, and we're getting local authors to read to the kids."

"Oh, God no," Megan gasped.

"So I was wondering if you had anything appropriate for, let's say, middle school English students, that you could read to them."

"Something I've written myself?" I asked, my excitement rising.

"That would be the idea."

"You don't know what you're saying," said Meg.

"Would it have to be published?"

"Ideally," said Karen. "But not necessarily."

"I don't have anything published yet, but I do have a rather good detective story I'm working on. It could be a pre-publication reading. A world premiere!"

"And could you bring that old typewriter in?" asked Karen. "And some of Chandler's books? They'd really get a kick out of it."

"Why, I'd love to," I said as Meg looked on in horror. "When am I scheduled?"

"In a few weeks. I'll let you know. Right now I'm just lining everyone up. I'm trying to get hold of Jan Karon, but I have to go through her agent. She's right up there in Blowing Rock."

"You're not really going to inflict your story on the English class are you? Could you be so cruel?" Meg asked as we left Dr. Dougherty to her soup.

"It will be a good experience for them."

"In what way?"

"Perhaps I'll inspire a few of them and they'll decide on a career in the literary arts."

"Or psychiatry."

Chapter 8

The circus was dark; not sinister dark, although I
suppose it was, but theatrical dark; that is, closed
for the evening, which was why it was also dark when
we arrived.

Lilith motioned me into the elephant ring. I went
in slow--as slow as a Piggly Wiggly checker on
Double Coupon Friday. She walked behind me with her
gun in one hand and her snake in the other. The snake
had stopped singing, and I was fresh out of hamsters.

"You know," began Megan, looking through some pages I had
stacked on the desk just beside the lamp. "Just because you happen to have Raymond Chandler's typewriter doesn't mean you
have to use it. It could sit nicely on a pedestal in the foyer – sort
of like a shrine. Other mystery writers could come and pay hom-
age to it. Maybe type quick notes to their mothers."

"But think of the stories that would be lost to the world," I
said, the keys clacking in rhythm to an early Leadbelly recording.

"I prefer to think of the children," said Meg, "and the unborn
generations that may read this accidentally and be unduly affected
by your prose. Just because you own a gun doesn't mean you have
to shoot people."

"An unfair metaphor. Or is it a simile?"

"Maybe it's a dangling participle. Either way, you need to
stop – before someone gets hurt.

All geniuses had their critics. I ignored the insult and kept
typing.

"Take a right at the broken trapeze," she said.
"OK, Lilith," I said, "but remember that there are

71

people who will look for me when I don't show up in the morning. Now, what's your game?" I lit up a stogie.

"Why can't you love me? I know I'm a leper, but lepers have feelings, too."

"Not in their extremities, Lilith. And anyway, I'm seeing someone." Sure I was lying. Lying like a dead possum, or one pretending to be, but I wasn't going to try to romance my way out of this one. When I counted up all the lips in the room, I came up with five including the snake; and the snake had two.

"Who is she?" she said using venomous overtones, overtones that made Rolf pucker up expectantly. "Some soprano I suppose. You were always a sucker for a nice pair of lungs in a push-up choir robe." She waved the gun in my direction, gave Rolf a kiss on the snout and waited for my answer.

"Her name is Rocki. Rocki Pilates."

"The bishop's personal trainer?"

I was surprised. "You know her?"

"Who doesn't? She skates around plenty. She's not what you need, you know. She won't treat you right."

"No one treats me right."

"Guess what?" Meg was not really in a "guess what" mood, so her "guess what?" was not so much a question as an introduction to her next comment.

"I met her today and, believe it or not, she's worse than he is."

"'Her' being?"

"Jelly Barna."

"Jelly Barna?"

Meg crossed her arms and continued in exasperation.

"The priest's wife."

"Her name is Jelly Barna?"

"Listen, will you. This is serious."

"OK," I said. "What's up?"

Meg sat down at the table. "Jelly Barna has been appointed the head of the Altar Guild by her husband. It's her 'gift.' So, as the head of the Altar Guild, she has taken it upon herself to call Christopher Lloyd in Boone."

"Mr. Christopher? The wedding coordinator?"

"It seems," she continued, "that Mr. Christopher is an expert in Feng Shui and will be advising us on the placement of furniture, the colors we should be using, and the arrangement of the flow of positive energy within the church. We will now be known as the Feng Shui Altar Guild and Jelly Barna is planning on using our church as a model throughout the diocese. They even have a web-site up already. It has *her* picture on it."

"And me still in the middle of Lent."

"You have to do something."

"Nope. I'm staying out of it. Till Easter anyway."

"We may be ruined by then."

"Well, do what you can to hold the heathens at bay," I said. "I'm getting another beer."

"Any word when you might be able to make it over?" It was Hugh on the phone.

"How about a week from Monday?" I said. "I have a Clown Eucharist to play."

"A what?"

"A Clown Eucharist. Surely they have them in all the great cathedrals of England."

"You're not serious? We do have a fellow who goes around to

churches dressed as a clown. He's quite popular. I can't remember his name."

"Oh, but I am serious. Lent is just too darn grim and we need to find our Inner Clown."

"Well, don't tell the clergy over here. The next thing you know..."

"I'll keep it our dark and terrible secret. How's the investigation coming?" I asked.

"I think they've forgotten about it. Out of sight, out of mind, you know. Now that the furor has died down, and since he, er...she was an American, we've all mostly put the unpleasantness behind us. Except for the little matter of the diamond."

"What about insurance?"

"That's the reason I'm calling. The Ecclesiastical Insurance Group was going to have to pay the Minster about 1.3 million pounds. I spoke with one of the agents and he indicated that since the video cameras were turned off and the other security measures disengaged, that there was a good chance that they would not pay."

"Ouch."

"That being the case, the Dean and Chapter have decided to offer a reward for the return of the diamond. Ten thousand pounds sterling."

"Ten thousand pounds." I mentally did the math. "That's better than fifteen thousand dollars."

"Closer to seventeen. Interested?"

"Why yes I am. What about you?"

"I'm employed by the Minster and therefore not eligible. There are another couple of privately funded fellows nosing around though."

"I'll bet. I'm guessing then that the next trip won't be on the Minster's tab."

"Nope. Sorry. All yours."

"OK, but I'm not going back to flying coach."

"Welcome to this program of the Lenten Institute," I said to the fifteen or so people gathered in the upstairs Adult Sunday School room. "If you're looking for the 'Finding Your Inner Clown' class, it's in the sanctuary."

There were a few sniggers from the back of the room, coming mostly, I suspected, from choir members who were looking for somewhere to land before choir practice began. We generally had a church-wide supper every Wednesday during Advent and Lent, followed by a brief program. Choir practice was last on the agenda, with everything finishing up around 8:30 or so.

"The program this evening is on Comparative Religions, and to that end I've called two of my friends from Asheville to be presenters this evening. Our first guest is Mr. Julian Mayberry from the Raelian Center of Appalachia."

Mr. Mayberry stood as I read off the card he had handed me earlier.

"The Raelian Revolution, the world's largest UFO related, non-profit, religious organization, has over 60,000 members in 90 countries. The Raelians are working towards building the first embassy to welcome people from space while sweeping the world with a fearlessly individualistic philosophy of non-conformism."

"Mr. Mayberry," I said. "Why don't you tell us about your views and how you came to the Raelian religion."

Julian Mayberry took the floor. He was a slightly built man, balding with old-fashioned, horn-rimmed glasses. His real name was Will Purser, and he was on the theater faculty at Lees-McRae College in Banner Elk. I only hoped he'd done his homework.

Julian Mayberry, a.k.a. Will Purser, pulled a three by five

index card from the inside pocket of his tweed jacket, adjusted his glasses, cleared his throat and began to read nervously.

"The Raelians were founded," he read in a quavering voice, "in 1973 by our father, Rael. He teaches us that aliens told the story of the Bible to ancient man, but because they were so primitive, they worshipped the aliens as gods also. How does Rael know this?"

He looked around the room as if expecting an answer, but everyone was sitting stock still, their mouths hanging open.

"Because the aliens told him, of course!" He let out a high pitched little squeal of joy that I took to be a laugh.

Julian Mayberry was nothing like the Will I knew. Will was a serious, confident man with a moderated, low-pitched voice, inclined to smiling for no apparent reason, and slow and deliberate in his speech. Julian, in contrast, was a nervous, twittering fellow that reminded me, more than anyone else, of Don Knotts in his heyday. Perhaps that's the character Will was drawing from – Julian's fictitious last name being Mayberry.

Julian continued, "The aliens also told him that we were created using DNA from scientists from another world and that they'll be needing an embassy when they land in Quebec. We have about half the money raised to fund the building of the embassy."

"Now you know, Mr. Mayberry," I said, true to the script, "that we are Episcopalian and find all this sort of far-fetched. Is there anything Biblically based about the Raelian Religion?"

"I'm glad you asked. I can prove quite conclusively that aliens are at work in the Biblical writings."

"Really?"

"In Matthew, I think," he said, putting the first card in his side pocket and pulling another from the inside of his jacket. "No, John. Here it is. John 10:16. 'I have other sheep that are not of this sheep pen.' Here Jesus is obviously talking about aliens."

"In that particular passage," I said, "we feel that he's talking about the Gentiles."

"That's one interpretation, I suppose," he said sullenly. "What about this then?"

He pulled yet another card from his jacket.

"In the Old Testament, it says that Gepetto was swallowed by a whale."

"By a great fish, actually," I said. "And I believe it was Jonah."

"Fine! By a great fish then. The point is that if Jonah was in the belly of a great fish for three days and nights, he would suffocate."

"I concede the point," I said.

"Not only that," he said, flipping his card over and quickly scanning the second side, presumably to get his facts right. "Jonah says in verse six, 'I went down and saw the bottoms of the mountains...' Now how could Jonah possibly see the bottoms of the mountains if he was inside the fish? Unless..." He paused, looking smugly around the room.

"Unless," he squeaked excitedly. "Unless the FISH HAD WINDOWS! You see, it couldn't really be a fish at all, but something that Jonah, in his limited experience with extra-terrestrial beings, took to be a fish, but was, in reality, a spaceship. Possibly Egyptian."

Most of the class had caught on by this time and were giggling loudly. The few remaining folks, still oblivious to the ruse, were trying to hush them up in a useless effort to remain polite to our guest.

Julian pulled out yet another card and continued.

"Obviously the Old Testament contains many direct references to aliens. In fact, the word 'alien' occurs no fewer than one hundred seven times in the New International Version alone."

"One reason that these strange and wondrous beings may

be hesitant to come forward now is found in Exodus 12:48. 'An alien living among you who wants to celebrate the Lord's Passover must have all the males in his household circumcised.' We of the Raelian religion feel that circumcising aliens would not be in our best interest. And any alien that has been circumcised by mistake should be duly compensated. To that end, we have begun a movement to re-grow our foreskins for implantation to the aliens when they arrive."

This was greeted with howls of laughter as Brother Julian adjusted his glasses.

"What's going on up here?" said a stern voice belonging to Father Barna. He had just left the other workshop to check on my progress.

"We're finding our inner clown," said Meg, wiping tears from her eyes.

The priest left with a scowl on his face. It was a good probability that Princess Foo-Foo was having a lot less fun than we were.

"Our next guest," I continued, "is Brother Harley Ray Hammond from the Apostolic Four-Square Pentecostal Holiness Temple of God with Signs Following. Brother Harley Ray?"

"Aw crap," came a voice from the back of the room.

"Is there a problem, Brother Harley Ray?"

"Call me Harl."

"Is there a problem, Harl?" I asked. Everyone had turned around in their seats to look.

"Yep," said Harl. "It seems like, in all the ruckus, my snakes has ekscaped."

The choir gathered for rehearsal in the loft, most of them still laughing.

"What about the snakes?" asked Christina Zordel, one of our new altos. "It's not that I'm scared of snakes. It's just that I don't want them to sneak up on me. Especially rattlesnakes."

"Well *I'm* scared of snakes," said Rebecca Watts, near panic. "Was he kidding? I thought he was kidding! He let rattlesnakes out? I thought he was kidding!"

"I don't think they're actually rattlesnakes," I said, trying to calm Rebecca down.

"What kind are they?" asked Beverly, "And how many?"

"There were two," I said. "Maybe three. Four, tops...Ok, five that got away. They're Eastern Hognose snakes. They're totally harmless, but they look very much like rattlesnakes. They were part of Harley Ray's presentation."

"Hognose snakes are quite timid," said Fred May from the back row. "I used to keep them when I was a kid. They'll even play dead if they feel threatened."

"If I see one, it had better *be* dead!" said Rebecca.

"I'm sure they'll all be rounded up by tomorrow," I said, trying to still the restless waters. "The pest control folks are coming in. They're very thorough. Now let's look at the anthem for Sunday. Of course, a week from Sunday there will be something completely different."

"We really like your detective story," said Georgia, changing the subject and pulling several chapters out of her folder. "It makes for good reading during the service. I'm taking mine home so Dewayne can read it."

"Please don't encourage him," said Meg. "He'll just keep writing."

"I hear you're giving a reading to an English class," said Fred.

Meg's head dropped into her hands.

"Why, yes I am. I'm hoping to inspire them."

"Aren't we going to rehearse the clown anthems?" asked Christina, changing the subject again.

"I don't think there are actually any clown anthems. At least I haven't been informed that there are."

Christina smiled. I could see she knew something that she wasn't telling.

"OK," I said. "Spill it."

"Well, I heard," she began in her tell-all voice, "that Shea Maxwell is going to sing *Send in the Clowns* for communion. Only with different words."

"Really," I said. "No one's given me any music for that."

"Oh, you won't need it," said Beverly. "She's using an accompaniment CD."

The entire choir laughed as my head hit the console of the organ with a loud thump.

"Am I the only one who didn't know about this?"

The entire choir nodded.

"We found out at dinner," said Christina. "Shea was quite excited. She says that you never ask her to sing solos, but Princess...uh...Brenda was happy to include her in the program."

"Ah well. Let's work on something suitably depressing then," I said. "Pull out the Mozart *Ave Verum* please."

"Why do they use snakes anyway?" asked Rebecca as anthems ruffled in the folders.

"Mark 16:18 — 'they will pick up snakes with their hands; and when they drink deadly poison, it will not hurt them at all...' Some denominations take it literally. At least some of the ones in the hills," I explained. I didn't really have this scripture memorized but Harley Ray and I had talked about it beforehand and decided that his real rattlers weren't a good idea. "Yep. They take it literally."

"And do *you* take it literally?" asked Meg.

"Absolutely. The Bible says 'they will take up snakes.' *They.* Not *me.*"

On Saturday morning, at precisely six o'clock, my phone started ringing. I picked it up only because I knew who was on the other end.

"Hi, Nancy. Any luck? Can the cows sleep safely in St. Germaine once more?"

"I heard that you skipped the conference in Atlanta," Nancy said. "And, yeah. We caught the tippers. We had dozed off, but the donkey woke us all up."

"Anyone we know?"

"They were kids from a fraternity at Appalachian State. A rush prank."

"Did you haul them in?" I asked.

"No," she said. "They were a bunch of scared freshmen. Dave and I got their names and sent them back to school with a warning. They won't be back. Connie Ray wanted to shoot them on the spot."

"Maybe you should have let him shoot just one as a warning to the others."

"Go back to sleep, boss. We'll see you Monday."

I heard Meg plundering the kitchen cabinets as I stepped out of the shower, dried off and stepped onto my digital scale.

"Oh no!" I yelled, loudly enough for Meg to hear.

"What's wrong?"

I came out in my robe and sat at the table.

"Bad news," I said, glumly. "I got on the digital scale and the number came up six-six-six. This is a Very Highly Advanced Digital Scale. It can't be wrong."

"You're lucky that it isn't a Very Highly Advanced Digital *Talking* Scale. Otherwise you'd have heard 'Congratulations! You have lost two pounds and you are the Antichrist.'"

"Here," I said, ushering her toward the bathroom. "You try it."

"Weighing in is a private thing between a woman and her scale. I'll thank you to close the door."

The door opened a moment later and Meg stepped out with a smile on her face.

"Your scale says that I'm three pounds lighter than last week and that I have a lovely disposition."

"Only because it didn't say you had *gained* three pounds."

"Scales have feelings, too," she said. "By the way, it also said to tell you that you are not really the Antichrist and it was just horsing around."

"That's even worse."

"Worse?"

"Maybe I actually do weigh six hundred sixty-six pounds."

Meg had breakfast on the table by the time I was dressed. Archimedes had perched himself on a cookbook and was eyeing a limp mouse that Meg had placed on his saucer. Baxter was outside worrying a squirrel that had taken refuge in the barn, his barks echoing across the field.

"Well, it's Monday. How is the Clown Eucharist shaping up?" she asked, feigning indifference even though I could tell she was eager for some gossip.

"I'll trade you information," I said. "I'll tell you about the clowns if you spill about the Feng Shui Altar Guild."

"Fair enough," she said eagerly and put down her fork. "Here's the latest. Mr. Christopher has decided to move the altar to the center of the church – right where the nave crosses the transepts.

The idea is to put pews on three sides and face the altar but to avoid offending the rooster."

"How do we avoid offending the rooster?"

"I'm so glad you asked. Each month has a different ruling animal. In March, that's the rabbit – but the rabbit is ruled by the animal sitting directly opposite. And that's the rooster. He sits in the west."

"Of course he does," I agreed.

"So we must avoid moving toward the west. Hence, the pews will be facing the other three directions."

"And we change these every month?"

"Yep. Next month the dragon is in his seat and we must avoid the dog. Also, we must place two statues of St. Francis on the front steps to attract the chi into the building."

"Why St. Francis?"

"They're the only ones that Mr. Christopher has for sale at his shop."

"Ahhh."

He says it will help the energy flow to the building. Also, he says that purple is no good for Lent. The color needs to be yellow or light green to promote healing and a feeling of calm."

"That sounds very special. I'm calmer already."

"Now how about those clowns?"

"Well, I'm supposed to write the opening hymn."

"WHAT!?"

"I told Brenda I'd be happy to write the opening hymn."

"Doesn't she know about *The Penguin of Bethlehem*?"[1]

"Apparently not," I said with an innocent look on my face.

"Have you written it yet?"

"Not yet. I think I'll do it the night before and sneak an insert into all the bulletins on Saturday."

"I'm beginning to think the scale was right after all."

[1] see *The Alto Wore Tweed*

Chapter 9

Chapter 9

"There's a woman to see you, boss," called Dave.

"Is she beautiful?" I called back, knowing that it would embarrass Dave to no end.

"Um...I guess so."

"Well, by all means, send her in," I called back.

It took me a moment to place the face that was framed in the doorway.

"Lindsey?" I stood and extended my hand that she took and held a few moments longer than was necessary, then surprised me by pulling me across my desk and giving me a lingering kiss on the lips.

She smiled. "Hello, Hayden. How are you?"

"Better and better. Come in and sit. Can I get you a cup of coffee?"

"Sure. That'd be great," she said, settling into the only other chair in the office.

"Dave," I called out.

"Ours is sludge. I'll run down to the Slab," said Dave, poking his head into the office. "Do you want a Danish or something?"

"Yeah. Get a few, will you?"

"I'll be back in a bit."

"I'm surprised to see you," I said as I sat down. "Did you come all the way from Raleigh to publish my book?"

"Sadly, no," she said, laughing. "I had an opportunity to talk to a writer's workshop at Appalachian State, so I thought I'd drop by and see St. Germaine. And you, of course."

"Well, what do you think?" I asked, ignoring her second initiative as best I could.

"It's a lovely little village, isn't it?"

"We like it," I said, returning her smile. "After we have our coffee, I'll give you the grand tour."

"I'd like that very much. I don't have to be back to class until this afternoon. By the way, how did your investigation in York turn out? A happy conclusion?"

"I haven't figured it out yet. There was a diamond stolen as well as the murder."

"A diamond?"

"Thirty-two carats."

"Wow! Sounds like a girl's best friend. Did you find it?"

"No. But I think I know where it is."

"Really?"

"Yep. My plan is to go back over, pick it up, and be the hero."

"I would think that there'd be a lot of people looking for it."

I nodded. "I suspect so. But, if it's where I think it is, they won't find it."

"Well, good luck. I loved York, by the way."

"It's a great city. I always like visiting."

"When are you off?"

"Early next week. And how long will you be in town?"

"I'm in Boone until the weekend. I have to be back at work on Monday, but I thought I'd come and hear your service on Sunday morning."

"Well, about that..."

"Yes?"

"It's not exactly our usual service. Our interim priest has scheduled something out of the ordinary."

"That's all right. I'd like to hear you play."

"It's a clown service," I blurted out.

"A clown service?"

"I'm afraid so."

"Do you have to dress as a clown?"

"Nope. But, everyone else does."

"I grew up with clowns. It sounds like fun," Lindsey said as Dave came back in the front door, carrying three coffees and a bag of pastries.

I spent a couple of delightful hours taking Lindsey around the town before she took her leave and headed back to Boone.

"OK," said Meg later in the afternoon when she met me for a cup of tea. "Who is she and why are you showing her around town?"

"Wow! Word travels fast in this burg."

"Yes, it does. Now 'fess up."

"That was my literary agent."

"Uh huh."

"Well," I admitted. "Not exactly *my* literary agent. But certainly, *a* literary agent."

"Ah. The woman you met on the plane. What's she doing here?"

"She's at some writing conference at ASU. She just came by to say hello."

"Is she married?"

"Nope."

"I hate her."

"You don't even know her," I said. "She's very nice."

"No she's not," said Megan, sipping her tea. "She's after you."

"Really?"

"Watch your step, big boy."

I usually gave Marilyn the information for the bulletin on Thursdays and this week was no different. I sauntered in around ten and met her at her desk.

"How're things?" I asked. Marilyn looked a bit harried.

"Just fine," she said through clenched teeth. "Just fine."

I lowered my voice. "I think the selection committee is looking at resumés this evening. Hang in there."

"Thanks," she said sarcastically. "The Lord's work is never easy."

"Speaking of which, I have the music for Sunday."

"I'm typing the bulletin up now." She pointed to some scrawled notes on her desk. "Of course, I'll have to redo it since I can't quite read Brenda's scribbling. And this is worse." She held up a note with the words *From the Desk of the Reverend Emil Barna – God's Voice in Appalachia* printed at the top. His scratches were no better than Brenda's and if anything, even more incoherent.

"Mostly I've been going by old service bulletins and plugging their things in where I think they'll fit. They don't seem to notice."

"I had no idea. Well, good luck."

"You could help you know."

"That's why I'm here," I said, magnanimously pulling a typed sheet out of my pocket.

"Great, but that's not what I meant," she said bitterly, the usual enthusiasm missing from her voice. She sighed and took the paper from my hand. "Do you have the hymn written yet?"

"Not yet."

Her exasperation was evident. "Hayden, this is Thursday. I have to get the bulletin finished by this afternoon."

"Don't worry. I'm working on it. Just list the title and I'll put the words on an insert and get it in before Sunday."

"You promise?"

"Absolutely."

She looked at the paper. *"Crown Him You Many Clowns?"*

"Clever, eh?"

"And what's this processional? *Entry of the Gladiators* by..." She squinted her eyes and adjusted her glasses. "By Julius Fucik."

"That's the guy."

"Is this for real?"

"I assure you it is. When you're typing it up, don't leave any vowels out of his last name," I said.

She shook her head, still looking at the paper. "No, I won't. In fact, I may put in a few extra."

I didn't see Lindsey on Sunday morning. She called on Friday afternoon with her regrets and said she had to return to Durham a couple of days early. I must admit that I felt a sense of relief in the knowledge that Lindsey, at least, wouldn't be judging my musical ability by what was about to take place.

All the clowns were gathered in the sanctuary an hour before the service to go through their routines. Jelly Barna was dressed in a yellow outfit with a huge red fright wig and a great red nose. Her husband, the priest, was more of a tragic clown – an Emmett Kelly figure with a sad face painted on. The other clowns were variously arrayed and carrying parasols, rubber bats, giant flowers and several other clownish implements. Jelly Barna was leading the miming clowns in the story of the creation. Others were practicing riding their tricycles up and down the aisle. I knew they were parishioners of St. Barnabas, but I couldn't tell who was who because of the makeup.

The Clown-In-Charge, a professional clown known as Peppermint, was a friend of Father Barna and had performed several of these clown services before. There would be a processional, followed by a reading from the Book of Clowns–the creation story–that would be mimed by various participants using beach balls. The sermon was next, followed by communion. Sometime during the service, we would all find our inner clown and leave the service in joy to love and serve the Lord.

Peppermint, I found out, in addition to keeping everything running smoothly, was in charge of making balloon animals and handing them out to the children in the congregation during Father Barna's sermon on Noah's ark. All the children, as well as the clowns, were going to be instructed to come to the front steps, gather around the priest, listen to the sermon and laugh in innocent delight as Peppermint created his balloon magic.

"Where's our hymn?" asked a female clown who looked like something straight out of a Stephen King novel. I recognized the voice if not the face. Princess Foo-Foo was a little tense.

"I'm getting ready to go run it off. Don't worry. I'll have it ready. You know, you look a little scary."

"I don't know how to put clown makeup on for heaven's sake. I did the best I could."

"I'd stay in the back, if I were you," I said.

The prelude, which the bulletin had listed as *The Clown Imperial March* was straight from the Coronation of George VI. The choir, although not singing anything specific, had gathered in the choir loft to watch the festivities while Father Barna, in his purple and orange garb, stood at the front of the church and announced the call to worship.

"Let us praise the Lord with laughter."

The congregation responded: "With laughter and with a joyful heart."

At those fateful words I launched into the processional: *Entry of the Gladiators* (also known as the *Circus March*) that has been heard at the beginning of every Ringling Brother's extravaganza since the Big-Top made its appearance at the turn of the twentieth century. The fifteen or so clowns poured in from the back of the church, some riding their tricycles, some dancing, and some handing out plastic flowers to the rather stunned parishioners; stunned because, although everyone knew this was coming, the sight of fifteen clowns entering the church to a circus march proved to be somewhat unnerving.

One of my choir members, a child psychologist by profession, has since informed me that the fear of clowns ranks near the top of the phobia list for young children. I, myself, didn't actually hear the panicked screams very clearly because I was pretty involved in playing the processional, but Meg told me later that there were quite a few parents heading for the front doors clutching their terrorized youngsters.

As the furor subsided, the remaining congregation was instructed by Father Barna to open their bulletins and to join in singing the opening hymn – the hymn that a few unnamed choral co-conspirators had slipped into the bulletins during the rehearsal. It was a familiar tune, the original words "Crown Him with Many Crowns" having been replaced, and the choir sang out with great delight.

Crown Him you many clowns,
And laugh with holy glee;
We honk our rubber nose and find
A circus all for thee.
The greasepaint we would wear;
The costume so complete;
The flower squirting water fair
Upon our giant feet.

Crown Him your Inner clown
The Clown above the sky
And worship Him as you do best
Throwing a custard pie.
We drive our little cars,
And tell our jokes with flair,
Then hit ourselves with two-by-fours
To show thy mercy there.

Crown Him you many clowns,
And worship Him above
For in this circus we call life
He is the Clown of Love.
The ringmaster will crack
His whip to end the play;
Then punch your final ticket for
That clowny judgment day.

We finished with a rousing descant and full organ on the final stanza. It had already been decided that, after the first hymn, my work for the morning was finished until the postlude. The Princess and the Priest were using recorded music for the remainder of the service – a practice expressly forbidden by previous rectors of St. Barnabas. Our sound system in the church was minimal – just a little amplification for the readers and the priest. Trying to send music through it was akin to listening to a symphony over a CB radio. Yet, as bad as the sound was, it didn't compare to the hopeless bungling of amateur clowns miming the creation story. One of the clowns read the passage from Genesis to the congregation as the other members of the troupe were readying themselves and their props for the play.

I'm the first to admit that I'm not a fan of the art of mime.

93

However, unlike many of my friends, I do not hold with the notion that mimes should be shot on sight – at least not on a Sunday. They're certainly less irritating than telemarketers, and since there hasn't been a national "do not mime" list published, we have no legal recourse but to endure the mime as best we can. That being said, I *do* appreciate the talent it takes to manage to escape from an invisible box.

The song chosen by Princess Foo-Foo and the one playing on the sound system during the portrayal of creation was "The Rainbow Connection" sung by Muppet favorite, Kermit the Frog. One of the clowns, a Kermit puppet on his hand, came to the front of the steps and moved Kermit's mouth in time to the words. Most of the clowns danced around with giant beach balls held over their heads in some sort of manic cosmic interpretation of the beginning of the galaxy. One of them was gyrating wildly, trying to keep a hula-hoop rotating around her generous waist and portraying what most of us assumed to be Saturn. She was having a difficult time of it, her championship hula-hoop days obviously further behind her than her ample derriere.

"I didn't know that the creation story included the 'Big Bang Theory,' Meg said quietly to Bev who was sitting beside her on the front row.

"It doesn't."

"Then why do the planets keep bumping into each other?"

"They haven't had enough practice."

"I kind of like that striped planet," whispered Elaine Hixon to no one in particular. "It looks like Uranus."

At that, the entire choir burst into barely stifled laughter. Elaine immediately turned bright red.

"No, wait...I didn't mean...that just came out wrong...I meant Neptune. Oh, great. Now I'm going to hell."

"Someday, we'll find it, the rainbow connection," sang

Kermit, "the lovers, the dreamers and meeeee."

The mimes put down their beach balls to polite applause and Foo-Foo the Horror Clown moved to the lectern.

"If the children will please come to the front at this time and sit with the clowns, we have a special treat for you this morning."

No one moved.

"Children, please come to the front."

Most of the small children had left in terror at the beginning of the service. The remaining few were understandably apprehensive. Still no one moved.

"We have a special treat. Peppermint will be making balloon animals for you all." She had spoiled the surprise, but she was getting desperate. Peppermint started blowing up long, thin balloons and motioning to the kids. He was less threatening than Foo-Foo, but the children still weren't convinced.

If a sad clown's face can fall any further, Father Barna's did a swan-dive as soon as he saw Moosey and Bernadette coming down the aisle.

They almost made it to the front when Moosey spotted the first snake.

"You're in trouble, gumshoe."

It was the biggest understatement since Saint Lucy said, "Come up anytime--I'll keep an eye out for you." I stood at the edge of the center ring feeling as useless as a Republican in a steroid-free California gubernatorial race. Lilith motioned me toward the middle of the ring with her gun. The air hung heavy with the perfume of the circus--elephants, greasepaint and hot-buttered chimps.

"What's the game, Lilith? Who killed Canon Shannon Cannon?"

95

She didn't answer. She smiled. It was cruel, one-lipped smile that was somehow alluring and unnerving at the same time. I lit a cigar.

Suddenly, I was surrounded by them. Clowns. And it wasn't a bit funny.

Moosey pointed out the snake, curled up underneath the Gospel lectern, to Bernadette who let out a yell and ran back down the aisle into the arms of her mother. Moosey, on the other hand, enamored of any kind of snake, leaped on it and raised it aloft, holding it behind its head.

"I got it!" he crowed. "But there's another one." He pointed with his free hand toward a radiator against the wall by the Mary altar. He spotted it easily because it was moving and moving quickly.

"I thought the pest control people had found them all," Meg said, with an edge to her voice.

"Well, I didn't want to alarm you," I said. "They didn't find them all."

"And by that you mean...?"

"They didn't find any of them," I admitted.

Clowns scattered like duck-pins as the snake slithered across the floor directly toward Peppermint. There were several shrieks and what seemed, to the congregation, to be spontaneous dancing. Moosey was in the middle of the fray.

"I'll get him," he yelled. "Here," he said to Father Barna, "hold this one." He handed his snake to the priest who took it before he knew what was happening.

"Ahhhh! Yahhh gahhh wahhhhgaaa!" said the priest, holding the wiggling snake by the tail. To his credit, he didn't drop it, but in the commotion, his hairpiece had slipped badly and was now resting over one eye.

"Listen," said Georgia. "He's speaking in tongues. And his hair is loose."

One of the ushers, dressed as a clown as well, had made his way down to the front of the church. He took the snake from Father Barna, carefully holding it behind its head, and walked it down the center aisle, taking the time to show it to any interested parishioners of whom there were more than a few.

Meanwhile, Moosey had cornered the other snake against the modesty rail in front of the first pew. He raised it victoriously above his head.

"I've got 'im!" He looked around in triumph. "Hey. Where's the other one?"

One of the clowns pointed down the aisle at the departing usher.

"Wait up," hollered Moosey, holding his prize in both hands and running after the usher. "Them's MY snakes!"

Father Barna was still a bit shaky as he adjusted his toupee, sliding it back into its approximate position. "Now," he said, "we'll continue with the sermon." He looked around. "Where's Peppermint?"

Peppermint had disappeared.

"These are my friends," said Lilith in a voice so husky that it could have pulled a dogsled. "Let me introduce you."

Their giant rubber shoes were tapping in anticipation, slapping against the floor with that sound that a goldfish makes after leaping out of its bowl but before your mother finds it stuck to the linoleum, and as I gazed around the center ring at Mr. Pickles, Tonk-Tonk, Grabby, Cheezo, Honker and Uncle Winky, I remembered skipping the chapter in my Beginning

Detective's Handbook entitled "How To Subdue Six Homicidal Clowns" and realized I had made a terrible mistake. Quickly, I came up with a plan: a plan so simple, it reminded me of my brother-in-law Tim, but unlike Tim, this plan just might work.

"Let's talk," I said to Uncle Winky. "Maybe we can make a deal. The merger should leave cash enough for everyone. No need to get greedy."

"No deals today, flatfoot," growled Uncle Winky. "We don't care about the merger. This isn't what you think. The bishop is spearheading a petition to do away with the Ministry of Clowns and taking it to General Convention. If you're dead, you can't protect him."

"Gee, Uncle Winky. I thought clowns were jolly."

"Nah. You're thinking of the Fat Man. He's one tent over."

The sermon might have been better if Peppermint had been there. It seemed to be a re-telling of the Noah story with a roll call of some animals – giraffes, dogs, birds, horses and mice – we presumed would have been created from balloons and handed out to the children. As it was, it fell flat. Jelly Barna tried in desperation to make some sort of animal, but she couldn't get the second balloon inflated, so it ended up as a snake; the one animal we'd already seen.

Although we usually sang the communion settings, this morning it was all spoken, so I sat back and waited for the end of the service. I had decided that I didn't care to take communion on this particular Sunday. This decision was borne out as Shea Maxwell began her Karaoke rendition of *Send In The Clowns*.

Jesus loves you, Jesus loves me,
Jesus is up in the air, where I want to be;
Send in the clowns.

I couldn't listen to anymore so I snuck down the choir steps and out the front door for a breath of air. Moosey was sitting on the front steps holding a snake in each hand.

"This one's name is Piggy," he said, holding a snake aloft. "This one's Joe. Momma's comin' to get me. She'll be here in a bit."

"Maybe you'd better take those snakes over by the bushes. People will be coming out soon," I said.

"Aw, they're just hognoses. They wouldn't hurt nobody."

"Some folks don't like snakes, Moosey. If you want to keep them, go on and wait over by the bushes."

"OK."

I went back into the church and up the stairs to the loft just as Shea was finishing up.

Where are the clowns? There ought to be clowns;
Thank heavens! They're here.

Mercifully, there was no closing hymn and everyone filed out to the postlude, leaving me alone in the choir loft. As I finished up, I heard, from the front of the church, my name being called.

"Hayden!" It was Brenda and she was frantic.

"Yes?" I called back.

"You need to get down here right now. I think there's been an accident."

"I'm coming."

By the time I got to the sacristy, all the clowns were huddled together next to the bathroom.

"OK," I said. "Back up and let me have a look."

The sea of fright wigs and baggy pants parted to reveal a lone clown lying motionless, face up on the carpet. It was Peppermint.

"Did anyone touch anything?"

"Nothing," said Jelly Barna. "No one touched anything."

"Call 911 and get Nancy up here," I directed. Tell her to call an ambulance and get hold of the crime scene guys from Boone. Everyone, please go and wait in the parish hall. I need to talk to you all. Don't change your clothes and don't talk among your-selves." It was a charge that I knew would be ignored.

They filed out the back door of the sacristy, through the alley and into the parish hall building where the congregation was meeting for coffee. I knew it would be just a few moments before people found out what had happened and started coming back in. I locked the door to the sacristy and the back door to the church, hoping folks would take the hint, but there were other ways in and I couldn't cover them all.

I pulled out my cell phone and called directory assistance. A moment later I was, as I was informed, connected with my party at no additional cost.

"Hello?"

"Hi, there. It's Hayden."

"Hayden! To what do I owe this wonderful surprise?"

"I just wanted to make sure you got home safely."

"How sweet. The trip was just fine."

"How's the weather over there in Durham."

"Chilly, but sunny. Just the way I like it."

"That's great. Can you hang on a second?" I put my hand over the phone, then came back on a moment later. "Listen, some-thing just came up here. Can I call you back a bit later?"

"Sure. Bye now."

"Bye, Lindsey."

I looked at Peppermint. He lay on his back, his wig half off, and his eyes wide open. Stuffed in his mouth was the front half of a balloon animal. This clown had choked to death on a balloon wiener-dog. I looked closer. Curled around one giant rubber shoe was another of Harley Ray's snakes.

An accident? Maybe. But I didn't think so.

Chapter 10

"This is just great!" Pete Moss said sarcastically as he poured my coffee. "No crime in St. Germaine for fifty years. Then I'm elected mayor and we have two murders inside eight months." Pete was referring to the demise of Willie Boyd, a case that I had solved just after Christmas.

"That's the way it happens sometimes," said Nancy.

"Yeah. But both of them in the church? That's just creepy," said Noyleen, putting some family-style bowls of breakfast good-ies in the middle of the table where Dave, Nancy and I could all partake of the bounty. "That would never happen at First Baptist. We love everybody."

"You're right about that, Noyleen," I said, taking a big help-ing of grits. "That's the beauty of the Southern Baptists. They know how to avoid a scandal."

"Heard about the autopsy yet?" Dave said, eager to change the subject before Catholicism came up.

I nodded. "I called earlier and talked to Kent Murphee down in Boone."

"And how're things at the coroner's office?" asked Nancy.

"Slow. Anyway, he said that the preliminary cause of death is asphyxiation. But there's a contusion on the back of Peppermint's head, so either he hit it on the counter when he fell, or he was knocked unconscious before the balloon was stuffed in his mouth. I didn't see any blood on the counter, but that doesn't mean anything. The lab guys will find it if it's there."

"The only things heavy enough to do any damage, at least within grabbing distance, were a couple of brass flower urns next to the sink. No prints though. The Altar Guild keeps those urns polished and if one of them was used, I doubt that the murderer had time to wipe it off. He might have been wearing the gloves lying on the sink. There are a few pair of white cotton gloves in the sacristy that the ladies wear whenever they handle the brass to prevent tarnishing and preserve the finish. I don't think we'll get anything from the gloves, but I sent them down to the lab anyway."

Nancy, presuming correctly that our meeting had started, put down her fork, pulled out a yellow legal pad and began writing furiously.

"Name?" she asked.

"Peppermint's real name was Joseph Meyer. He lived in Chapel Hill although he'd moved there within the last two years. Before that, he listed a residence in Florida. He was a professional clown. I got his resumé from Brenda."

I pulled a sheet out of my pocket, unfolded it and laid it on the table between the platter of country ham and the bowl of fried apples.

"He actually taught courses at the Ringling Brothers Clown College in Venice."

"Italy?" asked Dave.

"Florida. He was forty-one years old, unmarried, and apparently made his living doing birthday parties and church services. I put a request in for his tax returns, so we'll know more about that later. I called the phone number he listed and got an answering machine. I couldn't find any next-of-kin. The Chapel Hill police are trying to find a relation."

I paused in my recitation. "That's all I have," I concluded. "Questions?"

"Any suspects?" asked Pete, wandering up.

"None."

"How 'bout your new girl-friend?" mumbled Nancy under her breath, not daring to look up.

"Careful," I said, in my most menacing, mind-your-own-business tone. "She's accounted for. She was back home in Durham."

"And you know this because...?"

" I checked."

"Well, it is a little odd. Her showing up and then this clown getting killed."

"I agree. That's why I checked."

"How about your dwarf?" said Dave.

"He's not *my* dwarf," I sighed. "I think he's been out of the country, but it wouldn't hurt to find out when he's getting back. I know he wasn't at church yesterday."

Nancy wrote it down, and I knew she'd follow up on it.

"That it?" I asked, looking around the table. "Let's finish this food then."

"By the way," said Dave. "Other than the obvious, how was the Clown Eucharist."

"It was the best one I've ever attended," I said. "Next time I'm making Nancy the Chief Clown. Apparently, it's a dangerous job."

"Be glad to," said Nancy, taking the last biscuit and patting the gun at her side. "Top billing, God willing."

It was a bad time to fly back to England, but I already had my tickets. I was tying up loose ends at the house when Nancy called in.

"Guess what?" she said.

"I'm all a-quiver with anticipation."

"Your dwarf flew in on Saturday night. He got back into town at about midnight."

"He's *not* my...oh, never mind. Saturday night, you say?"

"Yep," said Nancy. "You want me to bring him over for a chat?"

"Not yet. I'll talk to him when I get back on Thursday. Keep an eye on him though."

"Will do. Have a good trip."

Chapter 11

"You're either pro-clown or anti-clown," said Mr. Pickles, "and since you're working for the bishop, we know where you stand," which, at the moment, was in the middle of the center ring, surrounded by a nightmare of Ringlingian proportions.

They moved in like Yuppies into renovated Brownstones—or maybe loft apartments on the upper West side; not those cheap, rent-controlled lofts converted from old run-down warehouses, but the nice ones designed by radical feminist architects with hyphenated last names—their clownish teeth mimicking the sounds of a Portuguese castanet band in an all night Flamenco parlor. Suddenly, a shot rang out.

"Freeze, you mugs, or I'll fit you for wooden kimonos!" yelled Kit, Girl-Friday. "Now blow before I burn powder."

"Huh?" said Tonk-Tonk.

"You heard me. Breeze, ya bunch of daisies, or I squirt metal. Go climb up your thumb before I show you the Harlem sunset."

The clowns looked confused.

"I think she'd prefer you leave," I said, translating. "You too, Lilith."

Lilith took her snake and spun on her heel, or what was left of it.

"This ain't over, shamus. We'll be back."

The flight to England was uneventful, although tiring. I took the opportunity to work on my literary masterpiece, knowing that Lent was coming to an end and I had to finish up. But writing on the laptop didn't give me the same feeling as typing on the old man's typewriter. When using his typewriter, I felt an affinity with Chandler that the iBook didn't communicate. I'd re-type it all when I got home, of course, but the experience was incomplete – cheapened by technology. I closed the computer and thought hard about the case at hand.

Kris Toth, a songman at York Minster, had been killed; strangled after having been knocked unconscious. Kris had been studying on a fellowship and a position as a baritone in the Minster choir. Slender, with medium length black hair and a good-looking beard, Kris was by all accounts a pretty good baritone despite the interesting fact that he was a she. She was strangled with her own pair of black pantyhose.

The autopsy revealed that Kris Toth suffered from hirsutism, a condition described to me, a layman, as one in which too much hair grows on a woman's face or body. Hirsutism, which runs in families, can be caused by hair follicles that are overly sensitive to male hormones (called androgens) or it can be caused by abnormally high levels of these hormones. These levels may also be caused by tumors, but this wasn't the case with Kris, her pathology being termed "idiopathic hirsutism." She was apparently very healthy when she was killed. There are treatments or, at least, cosmetic remedies for the condition, but Kris chose to remain bearded.

She was found, dead, wearing a Victoria's Secret outfit underneath her choir robe and clutching a pectoral cross, in the middle of the Roman ruins. The case that had contained the cross also contained a chalice containing a flawless, 32-carat diamond.

Presumably, an accomplice killed her. The fourth finger of her right hand was Superglued to her thumb.

The provenance of the cross was interesting. It was thought to have been worn by Czar Nicholas II when he was assassinated in 1918. Valuable, of course, but nothing compared to the diamond set in the chalice, which was subsequently discovered to be missing and replaced with a CZ that had been super-glued into place. The missing diamond was insured for 1.3 million pounds, but the insurance company didn't want to pay.

The video surveillance had been turned off by persons unknown sometime during the forty minutes in which the Evensong took place. Kris Toth had left the service about halfway through and didn't return. Other choir members thought she was feeling ill. The reason that the Minster Police hadn't noticed the problem with the cameras was that the policeman on duty had a daughter singing in the choir, and he had stepped into the church to hear her solo.

There were a couple of problems. Why, if Kris was simply trying to steal the diamond, would she take the cross as well? The diamond had been replaced, and if she had left the cross and walked out, no one would have been the wiser. Replacing the diamond with a cubic zirconium might not have been discovered for years, but taking the cross almost guaranteed that she'd have been caught. She'd left the service in an obvious fashion. The cameras were turned off. She'd be the prime suspect in the theft. It appeared to me that the murderer placed the cross in Kris' hand after she was dead, locked the case and then left. One question remained. Did the murderer also get away with the diamond? I thought not.

If the murderer had taken the diamond, the logical thing for him to do would be to kill Kris and escape, leaving all the cases intact and locked; not drawing attention to any single one in particular. A murder in the Minster would be horrible, but would be forgotten soon enough. As it was, I suspected the murderer used the cross as a method of drawing attention not away from the chalice, but *toward* it, intending that we would indeed discover the substitution. If this was his intent, then the murderer was still expecting to be able to recover the diamond and was counting on someone to lead him to it. That someone was me, and this made it all very personal.

The train pulled into York twenty hours after I left St. Germaine, and I was still groggy despite having caught a few winks off and on during the journey. I made my way through town, then stopped at the Minster School to say hello to the headmaster, Geoffrey Chester. Geoffrey had helped me in my last murder case and I always stopped in to say hello.

"Need any help on this one?" he asked.

"Absolutely," I said. "What do you know?"

"Not a thing. It's mystery to everyone."

We chatted for a few moments before he rushed off to class. I made my way to Hugh's house, set my alarm for 4:30 and fell asleep in the guest room. Two hours later, I took a shower and, feeling refreshed, headed over to the Minster for Evensong.

The men and boys were singing. As I sat there in a church where the worship of God had taken place continuously for over eight hundred years, I closed my eyes and listened to the prayers, the psalms, the Thomas Tallis short service and the anthem – *Turn Thou us, O Good Lord* by William Child – and thought to myself, "You know, this place could really use a Clown Eucharist."

After the service, I met Hugh at the door to the sacristy.

"Good trip?"

"Fine," I answered. "Now, how about some dinner?"

"I know just the thing. We'll go and have a curry. Janet's still teaching. She said to meet her over at the school."

"That sounds great."

We made our way across the street to the Minster School.

"So," he said, lowering his voice. "Do you know where the diamond is?"

"I think so. When does the treasury open?"

"Tomorrow morning. Nine a.m."

"We'll be there at 7:30. We'll need a couple of Minster Policemen."

"You think the diamond is still in the treasury?"

"I do."

"7:30 it is then. I'll make a couple of calls."

Early the next morning, Hugh and I met Frank Worthington and George Ross by the side door. They were both off duty and clad in their civies rather than in their Minster Police uniforms. Although there were a few folks milling about the Minster when we entered, the hustle and bustle of cathedral business had not yet started. Frank had the key to the treasury and led us down the stairs.

"This is it." I said, stopping by the Roman well.

"What? Here?" asked George. "How do you figure?"

"I don't think the diamond ever made it out of the treasury. I might be wrong, but I'll bet that it's right here. People throw coins in the well all the time, but a diamond could be dropped in and never found unless you knew where to look. It would be invisible in the water. My theory is that Kris either dropped the diamond in before the murderer knew it, or it fell in and the murderer didn't have time to find it before he had to leave."

"Of course!" said Frank. "We never thought to look. We clean out the coins every couple of months, but unless we stepped on it, we'd never notice the diamond. We all presumed that it was taken by the murderer."

"It could've been, but I don't think so. I don't think it ever made it out. Let's check the well."

The Roman well is quite shallow and was easy to search. We were very thorough, first removing the coins, then submerging a one-foot square piece of stainless steel mesh cloth I had brought and laying it flat on the floor of the well. The well was only three feet across, and we all strained to see any anomalies in the surface of the metal cloth as it rested on the bottom. We looked for about thirty minutes, going over each section several times before finally abandoning the cloth and running our hands over the bottom of the well. We then turned our attention to the shallow stone drainage channel close at hand, also built by the legionnaires, which had a stream of water running through it from an outside source. We checked the drain, making sure that the diamond could not have been flushed through, then conducted our examination again, going over the sunken stones with the mesh first and then with our hands. The only thing I found was a broken piece of glass that I inadvertently dragged my hand over.

".Jeez!" I said, pulling the jagged shard of clear glass from channel and inspecting the palm of my hand. There was a pretty good-sized cut across the palm. It wasn't deep and it looked to be clean.

"Go on up to the station," said Frank. "They have a first aid kit. It doesn't look too bad. They can probably fix you up."

"Thanks."

I went upstairs and got bandaged. We searched for another hour, but in the end we were all convinced that the diamond was not there.

"Rats."

"Too bad it wasn't there," said Janet. "Finding it would have paid for your trip."

"Yeah, I guess." I was in a foul temper, and my tone was none too cordial.

"We're eating tonight at Falconthorpe," said Hugh, trying to cheer me up.

Immediately my mood lightened. "That's great. Then the trip will have been worth it."

"It's just you two," said Janet. " I hate to miss it, but I have a parents' meeting."

Janet and I spent the rest of the day shopping. I had promised several people that I'd make an effort to return with some goodies, and to that end Meg had made me a list. This list included various teas and a scone mix for Anne Cooke, souvenirs for the gang at The Slab, and the mention of "a very nice gift for 'someone special.'" We finished late in the afternoon and made it back to the Minster for Evensong. I wasn't familiar with the Whitlock fauxbourdon settings of the Evening Service, but I'd seen them on the schedule and, although I wouldn't have missed the service, it was an extra treat to hear something new. After the service, Janet said goodbye and headed back to the school. I met Hugh at his Porsche.

"Do you mind if I drive?" I asked, climbing into the driver's side before he could object too strongly. "You're insured, right?"

The sun was low in the sky when we left York, our drive taking us away from the city, winding through small townships connected by roads no wider than an average American driveway. I noticed Hugh's fingers digging into the armrests as I dodged some, but not all, of the unwary pheasants that crossed our path heedless of oncoming traffic. He got mildly upset when I ran a couple of on-coming tractors off the road and he made some mention of my speed – albeit, through gritted teeth – as I took the last stone bridge doing seventy. Forty minutes later we pulled into the lane leading to Falconthorpe, a beautiful medieval manor house. It was almost dark when we crossed the moat and pulled through the gates.

"Did you notice that I didn't hit any of the black swans?" I said proudly, turning off the car.

"I'm very grateful," said Hugh, the tension of the trip evident in his voice. "I'm sure the swans are grateful as well. I trust that you will allow *me* to drive us home."

"If you insist."

We rang the bell and were greeted at the door by Martin Bensworth-Crowly and his wife, Lady Allyson.

"Ah, Hugh and Hayden. It's so good of you to come," said Martin graciously.

"Our pleasure, of course," replied Hugh, shaking hands. "How are you Martin? Allyson?"

"We're *very* well," said Martin, resplendent in his velvet smoking jacket. "And we trust you are the same?" Hugh nodded.

"We are so sorry that Janet couldn't come. But we're glad to have *you* with us again," said Lady Allyson, taking my hand in both of hers and clasping it warmly. It was all part of a graceful dance and one I enjoyed immensely.

"Thank you for your thoughtful invitation," I said. "By the way," I continued with a straight face, "Hugh wanted you to know that I didn't run over any of your swans."

Hugh blanched and rolled his eyes.

"You are *most* kind," said Lady Allyson elegantly, not missing a beat. "We hadn't planned to have swan on the menu until *next* week." She laughed and stepped back from the door, gesturing us inside. "Now come in out of the cold."

"Cretin!" hissed Hugh.

The door opened into the oldest part of the house, the undercroft of the Great Hall. Martin hung up our coats and we followed our hosts into the drawing room, a welcoming fire playing on the ancient stones adorned with ancestral portraits. The other four dinner guests had arrived earlier. I recognized one of them.

"Do you remember this old, retired bishop?" said Martin with a grin. "His Grace, Lord Horatio Biggerstaff."

"Of course," I said and shook his outstretched hand. "Your Grace."

"Call me 'Wiggles'. Everyone does."

"Wiggles, then. It's delightful to see you again."

"And you."

With introductions and refreshments offered all around, I hinted toward the possibility of a quick tour of the house. Martin, always proud to show off the manor, quickly agreed.

"You must tell me what you're working on," said Lady Allyson as we climbed the stairs to the Great Hall. "I find detective work just fascinating. Hugh has told us about the diamond."

"It will be my pleasure. I confess that I'm stuck. Perhaps you'd lend an ear."

"How marvelous," she said, her eyes sparkling. "I'd love to."

The party wandered through the Great Hall, Martin leading the way and pointing out details to the guests. Lady Allyson and I brought up the rear. We paused by the entrance and I explained my analysis of the Kris Toth case. I covered my theory of the missing diamond and ended with the account of our fruitless search. This concise explanation was for my own benefit as well as hers. I wanted to get all my facts in order.

"I'm sure you're right about the diamond," she said. "And it wasn't in the Roman well?"

"No, it wasn't."

"And that's where you cut your hand?"

I looked at my palm with the bandage around it and nodded. " I dragged it over a piece of a broken jar. It was transparent in the water. The Minster Police station had a first aid kit, so they bandaged it up for me."

"Was it a bad cut?"

"Not really. It wasn't very deep. They cleaned it, put some Dermabond on it and stuck it together. Then wrapped it up all nice and neat."

"Well, I'm very glad it wasn't worse."

We followed the group into the Chapel. Seeing that we were on holy ground, I told Lady Allyson about the Clown Eucharist.

"You're not serious?" she asked with a laugh.

"Those were Hugh's exact words, if I remember correctly. And if that weren't enough," I chuckled, "a clown named Peppermint choked to death on a balloon animal during the service. I'm sorry, I shouldn't be laughing. I know it isn't funny."

"Choked to death?"

"We think so. He was back in the sacristy. The offending balloon was a wiener-dog. And did I forget to mention our new verger?" I asked, continuing my litany of recent absurdities. "He's a dwarf named Wenceslas Kaszas. Our interim priest, Emil Barna, is an ex-lawyer who believes he's God's Voice in Appalachia and his wife, Jelly, has created the Feng Shui Altar Guild."

Lady Allyson laughed, then stopped abruptly, tilted her head slightly to the side and didn't speak for a long moment. "I think supper's ready," she finally said, taking my arm and leading me back to the stairs.

"What was the clown's real name?" she asked as we descended.

"Joseph Meyer."

She nodded and smiled as we came down the remaining stairs.

"Here's something you might find intriguing," she said when we returned to the drawing room. "All of the interesting people in your story are Hungarian."

I'm sure my face registered my astonishment. "Really?"

"Wenceslas Kaszas, Kris Toth, Emil Barna, Joseph Meyer; all Hungarian surnames. Forenames too, for that matter."

"I thought 'Meyer' was Jewish."

"It could be. There are several spellings. He could be Jewish as well as Hungarian. I'm just telling you that Meyer is a common Hungarian name. I don't know about 'Jelly.' It could be a nickname."

"Wow," I said, impressed. "How do you know all this?"

"My mother was Hungarian. Do you think it's a coincidence?"

"If it is, I'll eat my hat."

"Ah," she said smiling and ushering me into the dining room. "But we're having roast beef."

Chapter 12

I was as tired as a Streisand arrangement when I got back to the office. It was late--maybe too late. I unlocked the door, turned on the light and saw Rocki Pilates sitting in the chair behind my desk wearing only a smile and nibbling a watercress sandwich.

"Where do you get watercress this time of night?" I asked, wondering if she'd stick to the leather when she got up.

"Down at the all night condiment market," she said with a wiggle and a seductive smile. I hadn't seen that much wiggle since I invested all my retirement income in Jenny Craig's version of Martin Luther's "Diet of Worms." She peeled herself from the seat with the sound of a giant kiss. "How 'bout a taste?"

She sashayed toward me, tossing the half-eaten sandwich over her shoulder. Then she put her arms around me and puckered up like a Melanie Griffith on "Free Collagen Day" at the Beverly Hills Nip 'n Tuck.

"Take me," she panted, her bosom heaving like a sorority pledge on dollar beer night. I had to admit it, Rocki had a body like a brick rectory and a brain to match. But I wasn't buying it. I deftly executed a reverse suplex and tossed her onto the credenza.

"I know your game Rocki," I said as she picked up her clothes and started to dress. "And it sure isn't chest...er...chess."

"You're such a sexist," she huffed.

The insult hit me like a very light, almost imperceptible feather. It wasn't true. I had been to the bishop's weekend retreat on tolerance in the

workplace, and I had the bloodstained diploma to
prove it. Granted, I had been dragged into the
conference screeching like a gut-shot tenor, but once
I was handcuffed to the radiator, I settled down and
made the best of it. By Sunday night, I had a whole
new perspective on liberated women. I now supported a
woman's right to choose--either silicone or saline.

With my recent trip behind me and my jet-lag fading like
George Szell in the ninth, I was more than happy to kick my writing up a notch. I handed a couple of recent pages to Meg to pe-
ruse.

"OK," admitted Megan. "I have to admit it. You're getting
better. There are several sentences in here worthy of the Bulwer-
Lytton Fiction Contest."

"It's always been my dream to win the Grand Prize. It would
be the crowning glory to an otherwise lackluster vitae. Maybe I'll
send in a couple and see what happens."

"I think you should. How's your hand? I know you can type,
but can you play the organ?

"Almost as good as new. No problem."

"By the way, Karen called to see if you could do your reading
next Tuesday. Is your story ready for the kids?"

"Just about. A few finishing touches."

"That's good because I told her you'd be happy to." She smiled
a devilish smile.

"Any news from church that I don't know about?"

"The FOOSCHWAG is in full swing," said Megan. "I hope
you're happy about *that*."

" FOOSCHWAG?"

"The Feng Shui Altar Guild. Jelly says it's our new acronym."

"*You're* the one who told me to stay out of it. *You* said..."

"I take it all back. I admit it. I was wrong."

"Nice try. But I am content to keep Lent in my own way."

"You know," said Megan, "you're acting like a fooschwag."

"That may well be," I said, laughing and changing the subject. "How is the selection committee doing?"

"There are two priests we're looking at. We didn't get a whole lot of resumés in, but there are two good ones. One of them is a woman." She waited for my reaction.

"Fine with me."

"Really? After the last one, I thought you'd be against it."

"I'm not against women priests."

"I'm glad you feel that way," Megan said, giving me a kiss on the cheek. "Because she's the front runner at the moment. Some of the committee members are understandably hesitant."

"Understandably. Why is she the front runner, if I may ask?"

"Her background is in liturgics. She's older — in her early fifties I think. She's been a priest in several churches including being on staff at the National Cathedral. She taught briefly in one of the seminaries. I can't remember which one. And she has several books published."

"Married?"

"Widowed. Recently, I gather."

"And why, pray tell, does she want to come to St. Germaine?"

"Her parents live in Lenoir. They're both in their eighties, but still in pretty good health. She wants to be closer in case something happens."

"How about the other one?"

"He's about the same age. Fifty-two or three. He has a wife and two grown kids. Not as solid a resumé, but very personable. He's a wonderful speaker. He sent a videotape of one of his services and it was very impressive. The sermon was outstanding. He has a wonderful singing voice and can actually chant."

"That would be a nice change. Even Tony wasn't very accurate in the chant department."

"He's from Greensboro and is looking for a smaller parish."

"Either one sounds fine."

"We're interviewing the week after Easter. By the way – just so you know – Father Barna has thrown his hat into the ring as well. It seems he likes it here and thinks he'd be perfect for the job. We're getting a lot of pressure."

"Does he have any support on the vestry?"

She shrugged. "Some. You know how it works. He takes people out to lunch and asks for their advice. They feel important."

"I take it you don't approve?"

"It's the quickest way to split a church. I've seen it happen before."

"Well," I said. "Enough is enough. Maybe I can help."

I found Wenceslas at the church the next morning. He was coming out of Emil Barna's office as I made my way past Marilyn's desk.

"Good morning, Wenceslas," I said as cheerfully as I could.

"And a good morning to you sir," he said with a slight bow.

"I wonder if I could have a few words with you?"

"Of course," he replied. "Let us get some coffee and talk."

We walked into the empty parish hall where a pot of coffee was always waiting, poured ourselves a couple of cups and walked over to a table. Wenceslas produced a cushion, seemingly out of thin air, which he put on the chair before climbing up. I sat down across from him.

"I have a few questions for you, if you don't mind."

Wenceslas nodded, but his eyes narrowed.

I got right to it. "Did you happen to know the clown that was killed on Sunday?"

"Am I suspected of this killing?"

"I'm just trying to get all the facts," I said, shrugging my shoulders.

Wenceslas sighed and put his hands in his lap.

"I knew him, yes. He was a friend of Emil's. I knew him from the time I was the valet to Emil in Raleigh. He was called Joseph Meyer."

I nodded and took a sip of coffee. "You were out of the country last week?"

"I made a trip to Hungary. It was family business."

"When did you return?"

"On Saturday night. I arrived at my home at eleven in the evening. I was very tired and went to sleep."

"So you weren't here for the Clown Eucharist."

Wenceslas looked disgusted. "I was not. I do not like clowns." Then, considering his last statement, added, "But I do not wish to kill them."

"Yes, I can understand that. A mime, perhaps, but not a clown."

Wenceslas relaxed and laughed. "Yes, a mime, perhaps."

"How was Budapest?"

"I flew to Budapest, but I am not from there. I am from the town of Szentendre. That is where I went."

"Well then, how was Szentendre?" I asked. "I've never heard of it. What's it like?"

"It is beautiful." He smiled and looked every bit like a diminutive Santa Claus. His eyes twinkled as he described the winding roads, colorful houses and narrow back-alleys. "There are seven steeples," he said, holding up seven fingers, "and more museums than you can count. And the Danube...ah, the Danube..."

His voice trailed off as if he was being transported. "When I was a boy, we would perform on the banks of the Danube." Suddenly he snapped back to the present.

"You would enjoy Szentendre," he said, still smiling.

"I've never been to Hungary. It sounds as though it would be worth a trip, though."

"Be careful," said Wenceslas. "You might never want to return."

"You were a performer then?"

"In my younger days."

"A street performer?"

Wenceslas sat up straight and looked indignant. "The Kaszas family has entertained the crowned heads of Europe since Napoleon! Street performers! Bah!" Then he shook his head. "But socialism changed everything. I was ten when the war came."

"Did that put an end to the family business?" I asked.

"It was over much earlier," he admitted. "Before I was born. The Great War was the finish. Hungary chose the wrong side, you see."

"Ah yes," I nodded. "Hungary was an ally of Germany."

"Yes. It was too bad. The Kaszas family's last great performance was at the end of the war. A command performance. But, even by that time, many family members had come to America. Even my grandmother."

"Is Emil from Hungary as well?" I asked.

Suddenly Wenceslas was on his guard. "He is an American. I am Hungarian."

"When did you come over?"

"I arrived in this country two years ago. I am not a citizen. I have work papers."

"A green card."

"Yes."

"Why come to America?" I asked.

"It was a family matter."

"You have family over here?"

"I did, yes. They are gone now."

I got up and extended my hand. "Thank you, sir. I appreciate your talking with me. And I hope to see your home sometime in the near future."

"Take your lady friend," he said, smiling. "You will fall in love all over again."

"Did you see this?" Nancy said, pointing to an article in the paper.

"I haven't had time to read the paper," I said.

"Louisiana," she said, prefacing the story. "A policeman pulled over a Pontiac Grand Am outside Monroe. When he walked up, he noticed something amiss. He ordered them out of the car, and when they climbed out, they were all naked. Eight of them. Eight naked Pentecostals."

"That can't have been pretty. What was their story?" I asked.

"It seems that they believed the Second Coming was imminent. They thought their clothes were possessed, so they threw them out of the car around Alexandria."

"I've often felt the same way."

"So what do you think?"

"I think the Grand Am is a swell car. Any news from the crime lab?"

"As a matter of fact, yes. They swabbed every surface in the sacristy. They found traces of blood on one of the corners of the counter. He probably hit his head on the way down."

"So," I said, pausing a moment to think. "An accident?"

"Could be. But your dwarf is still unaccounted for. He arrived home Saturday night late. He wasn't at the service and no one saw him until about two in the afternoon on Sunday."

"Let's suppose that Wenceslas did want to kill him. I don't think the facts bear it out."

Nancy stopped perusing the paper and gave me her attention.

"Those urns have a nice edge to them. If he used one of them to knock the clown senseless before sticking the balloon down his throat, how did he reach Peppermint's head? There wasn't a stool or a chair in the sacristy. I doubt that he could have climbed onto the counter. Peppermint wasn't a small guy – about six feet tall I'd say. So unless, Wenceslas snuck up on him carrying a ladder and then taking it out afterward – a scenario which I find highly unlikely – I don't see how he could have done it."

"Not to mention that there wasn't any blood on the urns," Nancy added. "What if he had a long stick? Or a bat?"

"Maybe. But it was a cut on his head. Not blunt force trauma. Nope. I don't think it was the dwarf."

The FOOSCHWAG was in full swing when I showed up at St. Barnabas on Saturday afternoon. Meg wasn't in attendance, but I saw Mr. Christopher mincing down the center aisle. He was shouting at the fifteen or so volunteers.

"Stop! It's time to take a Luo Pan reading!"

Mr. Christopher stopped in the middle of the church where the nave intersected with the transepts, pulled a chart out of his fanny pack and started humming. The others soon mimicked his humming.

"The Luo Pan is a compass," he said, stopping suddenly. "It not only tells us the direction, but investigates the energy of each direction."

The FOOSCHWAG gathered around him, eagerly trying to see the Luo Pan at work.

Mr. Christopher then walked around the church amid the hushed whispers of his admirers. Finally returning to the center of the church, he pulled another chart from his pack, unfolded it and studied it for a long minute.

"The information found in the Luo Pan is condensed into the Bagua. The Bagua represents the journey of life and it will tells us what we need to know." The FOOSCHWAG held its collective breath.

"There!" he said and pointed to the West transept. "That is where the energy is flowing from. It is the home of the rabbit. The altar must therefore be placed..." He looked around as if deciding, then pointed the opposite direction. "There!" he cried. "In the house of the monkey!"

The FOOSCHWAG applauded.

"What about the rooster," I asked from the balcony when the adulation had died down. "I thought we didn't want to offend the rooster."

Jelly Barna looked up at me with contempt. Mr. Christopher decided to ignore me and continue with the new arrangements.

"Let's move the altar over there," he said, pointing to the East transept. We have to rearrange all the pews as well. Everything must point to the East."

I watched for a few more minutes, knowing that they'd have a bit of trouble with the altar. It had a marble top and probably weighed close to four hundred pounds. Unless they had a Feng Shui moving company stashed out back, they'd be at it for a while.

"The altar cloth, paraments and stoles must be changed as well," said Jelly. "I've had bright yellow ones made." She smiled at Mr. Christopher and he nodded his approval.

"Colors are nothing more than vibrations," said Mr.

Christopher. "Yellow will add to the Yang energy. Purple is the Yin. It's a bad color for the monkey."

I left on that note, heading back to the house and what I hoped was a peaceful Saturday afternoon.

Sunday morning was chaos. The processional had to be re-routed because the center aisle was now full of pews. The FOOSCHWAG hadn't been able to move the altar – at least on such short notice and with no moving equipment – so they had hidden it with a bamboo privacy screen and set up the elements for communion on a folding table they had brought in from the parish hall. Covering the table was an obviously handcrafted, bright yellow altar cloth with appliquéd chickens. Behind the table was the "water feature," a five-foot high fountain that, due to some plumbing problems, was spurting water only sporadically and making a noise like an intermittent whoopee cushion.

Although Jelly and Mr. Christopher were trying to direct traffic, the congregation was very confused; most of them were milling about when the service started. After all, many of them had sat in the same pew for generations and the rest of the parishioners certainly weren't prepared for the rearrangement. Wenceslas, clad in his black velvet verger's outfit, ostrich plume aloft, kept trying to point the acolytes and readers to their positions. They were, however, as lost as the congregation. Father Barna and his two attendants couldn't get through the crowd so the two boys finally dropped his train and retreated. This caused the priest to trip over his poultry-covered cope until, in disgust, he slung it over his shoulder like a Roman Senator. The choir, with no room to process, simply came up the stairs to the loft.

"Are those chickens?" Rebecca asked, pointing to the decorated paraments.

"We're in the house of the monkey," Megan answered in a

whisper loud enough for the entire choir to hear. "But we don't want to offend the rooster."

"This is insane," said Elaine. "How long can we keep this up?"

"There's an emergency vestry meeting right after church," said Meg. "Maybe we can put a stop to this."

"Let us worship the Lord in the beauty of His sanctuary," Father Barna called out.

"Fffrrrraaaap," said the fountain.

Instead of replying with the printed response, the entire congregation started laughing.

"I'm feeling pretty tranquil," said Marjorie, pulling her flask out of the hymnal rack. "This Fing-Schwing stuff must be workin'."

"That's the chi you're feeling," said Bob Solomon from the back row.

"It ain't the chi," said Marjorie, taking a swig.

Notes From The Choir Member's Handbook

Notes From The Choir Member's Handbook

Dear Choir,

Now that we have several new members, I am often asked, "Listen Hayden. Just what the heck are you talking about?" Admittedly, this query comes mostly from the tenor section; however it must be pointed out that being in the choir is a highly technical and demanding profession. The terms which we use in music are not readily found in normal, everyday life. For example:

The lilting counter-melody sung over the hymn by the higher voices is called:
    A) descant
    B) death chant
    C) LILTING? Hahahahahaha!

If you answered "C" you have the makings of a fine choir member for you are unusually perceptive.

In accordance with the Choir Members Handbook put out by the ICCM (International Congress of Church Musicians) Page 745, Section 56, par. 9 subsection 7B, it is my job to educate as well as to direct. These then are several definitions which you may find make your choir experience easier to understand.

Pizzacato	Literally "Cat Pizza" (see Choirmember handbook p. 458: Wednesday night pizza dinner) Anchovies optional.
Ritard	Well ... the bass section, mostly.
Mass Ordinary	A common musical error. As in "Hey, you really made a mass of that one!"
Mass Proper	An extraordinary musical error. As in "Hey, you really made a proper mass of that one!"

Mode	A key, reflecting a particular emotion. As in *"I can't sing that. I'm not in the mode."*
Parallel Organum	A method of musical gratification frowned on by early church fathers.
Faggott	A bassoon. Yes, a bassoon.
Camerata	A small camera.
Cantata	A small can.
Sonata	A small son.
Prelude	A small Japanese car.
Glockenspiel	A dark German beer. As in *"Hey, Jim-Bob, throw me another Glockenspiel!"*
Homophony	An irrational fear of bassoons.
Letcher Lines	*"Hey baby, what's your sign? Come to choir practice often?"*
Libretto	A soprano born in September. Usually highly compatible with a Saggitario. (See Letcher Lines)
Minuette	Roughly 52 seconds.
Tonic	What is generally enjoyed over ice after choir rehearsal.
Dominant	In a choral relationship, usually the alto.
Euphonium	A choir invitation. If they won't answer your letters, euphonium.
Augmentation	Special surgery for altos involving the implantation of falsettos.

Basso Obstinato	Recurring wrong notes in the bass section.
Basso Continuo	When the director can't get them to stop
Incomplete Cadence	Harmonius interruptus
Score	Sopranos 3, Tenors 0.
Riff	What happens when someone takes your choir robe.
Contralto	An alto who has been convicted
Polychoral Motet	Six parrots singing "Exultate Justi."
Aleatoric (Chance) Music	Music performed by the random selection of pitches and rhythms. Frequently found in the choir anthem.
Castrato	The highest male voice (some alteration required)
Étude	What comes right before the Beatitudes
Concerto Grosso	An accordion concert.
Glissando	What directly precedes the highest note of a descant.
Leitmotif	Like a regular motif, but less filling.
Polonaise	A condiment frequently put on a parrot sandwich.
Recapitulation	What usually happens after you eat a parrot sandwich.
Rondo	A popular sixties song as in *"Help, help me, Rondo."*

Theme	*"We hate this anthem."*
Theme and Variations	
	"We hate this anthem, the composer and all of the composer's relatives."
Sectional Harassment Lawsuit	
	What happens when the director suggests that the altos *"Sing from their diaphragms."*
French Overture	*"Pardon moi, madamoiselle. You have beautiful eyes."*
Sax and Violins	What there is too much of on television
Smorzando	The "All You Can Eat" Buffet at Luciano's
Fugue	A squabble — frequently found in the tenor section. *"You cain't sing that note! That uns mah note! Now we uns is agonna fugue!"*
Tenuto	Nine utos plus one
Grand Pause	What happens when the conductor loses his place
Perfect Pitch	Throwing a banjo into the dumpster without hitting the sides
Sacbut	A choral singer over 40.
Antiphonal	Leaving your answering machine on all the time
Countertenor	A man who is bi-sectional.
Cantus Firmus	A singer in good physical condidtion. As opposed to the "cantus phlabbious" (see sacbut)

Isorhythm	When the tenors sing a rhythm totally different than the rest of the choir. As in *"All our anthems sound isorhythmic."*
Chorale Partitas	Small choir get-togethers – frequently interrupted by the police.
Phantasy	An alto in a leather choir robe.
Virginal	An alto in a leather choir robe.

So, as you can clearly tell, music is a very difficult and complex subject which requires years and years of careful study.

Learn these definitions. They'll be on the test.

Chapter 13

Chapter 13

"It was Race," Rocki said as she opened the door on her way out. "He put me up to it." The door slammed shut quicker than a white man's application to the University of Michigan law school.

I knew Race. Father Race Rankle. We had a past of course. He was an old college buddy. We once opened and ran a very profitable Liturgical Charm School for beauty pageant contestants although we had to close up shop after a particularly bad fire-baton incident. I had told him to cut down on the hairspray, but he wouldn't listen. That poor girl's hair went up like Bananas Foster at a Pentecost breakfast. If the next girl's talent hadn't been gargling communion grape juice while singing "I Come To The Garden," we could have had a real disaster. Luckily she was able to spit enough juice on the other girl's head to quash the flames. But that was ancient history.

Rhiza and Malcolm Walker had invited Megan and me out to supper on Sunday night. Although they'd been separated since Christmas, Rhiza had decided to give Malcolm another chance because he said he still loved her, he agreed to go to marriage counseling and he was the richest man in four counties. I knew this because she called me and asked my advice. Rhiza and I went way back.

"How was the meeting?" I asked Malcolm and Meg over the second glass of wine.

Malcolm was the Senior Warden and Meg was on the vestry. Rhiza had been on the vestry last year but her term had ended in December.

Malcolm shook his head. "I called the bishop last week and told him what was going on. He was..." Malcolm paused. "Unsympathetic. It seems that the Christmas incident is still fresh in the minds of the diocesan offices. Until we call a new priest, we have to keep this one."

"Can you rein him in?" Rhiza asked.

"Not really," said Malcolm.

"Not only that," interrupted Meg, "but you wouldn't believe the support for his application. It's about a third of the vestry."

"The search committee will be interviewing right after Easter," said Malcolm.

The weather had finally broken and Monday dawned fair and brisk. There was that almost imperceptible hint of spring in the air, although the temperature hovered around forty degrees. Most of the patrons in the Slab were in sweaters, but some had even gone to shirtsleeves in utter defiance.

"I see that y'all are putting on a show," said Noylene as she poured coffee for Nancy, Dave and me.

"Who y'all?" I asked using the correct mountain grammar.

"Why, all y'all Episcopals. It's in the paper. A big ol' ad."

"Let me see that," I said. Pete reached across from an adjacent table and handed me a section of the *Watauga Democrat.* It was open to a half page ad in the Living section.

"Oh my," said Nancy, looking over my shoulder.

There, underneath the small ad announcing First Methodist's weekly activities was St. Barnabas Episcopal Church's announcement of the first ever *Edible Last Supper.*

"I've got to go," I said, getting up and grabbing a biscuit off my plate. "I'll see you back at the office."

"If you'd come to a staff meeting once in a while, you'd know what we are doing," said Brenda.

"The *Edible Last Supper*? That's the *stupidest* thing I've ever heard of! What are you thinking?" I was past being polite.

"You just get out!" she screamed.

I stormed out, still furious, and paused at Marilyn's desk. She got up and poured me a cup of coffee.

"She's seriously unbalanced," Marilyn whispered.

"Yep," I said, calming down and taking a deep breath. "Tell me about the *Edible Last Supper*."

"Remember when we did the Seder meal? It's sort of like that."

"It's this Wednesday?"

"Yep. Part of the Wednesday night programming. Brenda and Jelly are setting up a long table at the end of the hall. It's supposed to look exactly like DaVinci's *Last Supper*."

"Uh-huh."

"They were going to use real people as the disciples but they couldn't get enough volunteers so they're borrowing thirteen mannequins from Harrell's Department Store in Boone. They'll be posed and dressed like the painting." Marilyn smiled. "You know, you should really show up for staff meetings."

"Traditional Jewish food will be placed in front of each disciple. The people will walk past the Last Supper and take some food off each dish. Sort of like a Biblical buffet. The runners will be dressed up as Mary and Martha. It's their job to go back and forth from the kitchen to the table and refill the platters. As I understand it, there won't be any narration, but there will be soft music playing in the background. When people are finished they're supposed to go into the sanctuary for some meditation time."

"Who's bringing the food?"

"It's like a potluck. Dishes have been assigned so folks will know what to bring. There are some bitter herbs, unleavened bread, roast lamb – that sort of thing. They leave it in the kitchen and Mary and Martha serve it."

"My Lord," I said, shaking my head. "This is worse than *The Living Gobbler*."

"I remember that! That was great fun!"

"Yeah," I said with a grin. "The entire choir of Sand Creek Methodist dressed up like the four major food groups. But this..." I shook my head. "I've got to go back to work."

"Wait! I forgot to tell you about the Mary Magdalene Coffee Bar."

"Oh no."

"Yep," said Marilyn. "Four flavors of coffee plus a cappuccino machine. By the way, you *do* know about the donkey, don't you?"

"Donkey?"

Marilyn laughed out loud at my panicked look.

"Connie Ray bought a donkey a couple weeks ago."

"I know. It's a watch-donkey for his cows."

"Well, Father Barna found out about it and thought it would be a great idea to ride the poor beast of burden into church during the Palm Sunday Procession. Connie Ray's bringing it in on Sunday morning."

"Because?"

"Because Emil Barna is the living image of Jesus Christ, head and shepherd of the church to this congregation," said Marilyn demurely. "He explained it to me."

"That's all very well. But how will they be able to tell which one is the donkey?"

Megan and I met Karen at the middle school. I had my typewriter tucked under one arm and my manuscript under the other.
Meg was carrying four of my old Raymond Chandler books.

"Good morning," said Karen. "I see you brought the infa-
mous typewriter."

"I did."

"Well, you're right on time. Marty Nelson is waiting for us."

Karen led us through the halls and to an English classroom.
When we entered, the students stopped talking momentarily and
studied us for a moment before deciding to ignore the interruption and resume their banter. Their teacher, Mrs. Nelson, brought
them to attention a moment later.

"Take your seats please. We don't have a lot of time," she
said, bringing the class to order. "This is Chief Konig, from our
police department. Most of you know him."

I recognized a couple of the kids from some scrapes I'd been
called in on. Nothing serious. Seventh graders didn't get into too
much trouble. I knew almost all the rest of them by name. St.
Germaine is a small town.

"As you know, we're wrapping up our 'Bad Writing' contest
this week. The results will be published in the school paper and
we'll post them on the school's web-site. "

I glared at Meg. She just smiled innocently as Mrs. Nelson
continued.

"Chief Konig is the proud owner of a typewriter. Not just any
typewriter, but the very typewriter on which Raymond Chandler
used to write his novels. Chief?" Mrs. Nelson motioned to me. I
set the typewriter on her desk.

"Is that really Raymond Chandler's typewriter?" asked a boy
with blue hair and a do that would make a porcupine jealous.

"It is," I answered. "Do you know Raymond Chandler?" I

was a bit taken aback. I didn't think that seventh graders read hard-boiled detective novels.

"We knew you had his typewriter so we've been reading selective chapters," explained Mrs. Nelson, "We're examining good and bad writing styles."

"And how does he rate?" I asked somewhat defensively, determined to defend my muse.

"Raymond Chandler is the master of the descriptive simile. In context, he is without peer," said Anthony Hatteberg. He was sitting in one of the front desks. Mrs. Nelson nodded approvingly and continued.

"We've been assembling our favorite Chandlerism's. Would you like to hear some?"

I nodded as hands went up all over the classroom.

"Why don't we start here," Mrs. Nelson said, pointing to the front row, "and we'll make a game of it. The Chief will have to guess where the quote came from."

I nodded confidently. Chandler was my business.

A boy at the head of one of the aisles stood up and began the test. "It was a blonde, a blonde to make a bishop kick a hole in a stained glass window."

It was an easy one. "*Farewell, My Lovely,*" I said.

The next student stood, opened his book and read "To say she had a face that would have stopped a clock would have been to insult her. It would have stopped a runaway horse."

"*The Little Sister,*" I said, apprehensively, but the girl nodded with a smile and sat down.

"I was neat, clean, shaved and sober, and I didn't care who knew it."

"*The Big Sleep,*" I replied, still fairly certain that I was right. I was. The next student stood up.

"She opened a mouth like a firebucket and laughed. That

terminated my interest in her. I couldn't hear the laugh but the hole in her face when she unzipped her teeth was all I needed."

I knew I had read it, but where? I shook my head. "I'm sorry I can't remember. How about *Playback*?"

"No, sir," came the answer. "It's from *The Long Goodbye*."

"Three out of four," laughed Mrs. Nelson. "That's pretty good. But now Chief Konig is going to read us a bit of his writing and we're going to critique it for him."

I glared at Meg again. This was a set up if ever I saw one. I opened my notebook and read.

It was a dark and stormy night; dark, because the sun had just set like a giant flaming hen squatting upon her unkempt nest that was the gritty urban streets; stormy, because the weather had rolled in like an angry fat man driving his Rascal into a Ryan's Steak House and then finding out that the "all you can eat" dessert bar had an out-of-order frozen yogurt machine.

"Let's stop there," said Mrs. Nelson. "Who can tell me what's wrong with that sentence?"

Every hand in the room went up. This was going to be a long morning.

Chapter 14

Nancy met me in the office on Wednesday morning.

"Morning, boss. Here's the clown report from the coroner." She handed me a manila envelope and waited expectantly for me to open it.

"Just curious," she said, answering my quizzical look.

I pulled out the report and gave it a quick read, my eyes automatically jumping to the bottom line.

"The cause of death," I said, still reading, "was a heart attack."

"So someone choked him with a balloon wiener-dog and he had a heart attack?"

"Maybe. The back end of the balloon was stuck pretty far down his windpipe."

"Could have happened," Nancy observed.

"Yep. Also there were a significant number of ruptured alveoli and the surrounding capillaries."

Nancy waited for an explanation.

"The small sacs where the air is exchanged in the lungs. Plus a pretty good sized pnumothorax – a hole in his lung. Kent thinks that it might have been there for a while. He also had an advanced case of emphysema. And his blood work had traces of benzodiazepine. Not a full dosage though. Probably Valium." I looked up. "He was a clown. Maybe he was suffering from performance anxiety."

"All of which means what?" asked Nancy.

"I have no idea."

I arrived at the Parish Hall just before six o'clock. Parishioners were starting to gather outside the doors. I went over and stood by Malcolm and Rhiza and waited for Megan to arrive.

"We're not allowed inside yet," said Rhiza. "They're not quite ready."

"Did I tell you about the two applicants we have coming in after Easter?" Malcolm asked.

"Meg told me. Either one sounds pretty good."

Malcolm nodded. "I just hope that one of them works out. Here's Meg," he said nodding in her direction.

Megan walked up and gave me a kiss. "Sorry I'm late. I was supposed to bring some bitter herbs. Jelly suggested a nice horseradish sauce. I had to take it around to the back so they could sneak it into the kitchen. It's all very secretive."

At that moment the doors to the Parish Hall swung open and we were swept in with the rest of the attendees. At the front of the hall, as advertised, was a long table covered with a white tablecloth. Seated and standing at the table in various poses – reminiscent of, if not actually replicating DaVinci's *Last Supper* – were the twelve disciples with Jesus in the midst of them.

"Welcome to the *Edible Last Supper*," said Jelly Barna after we had all made our way indoors. "Please go through the line and then eat reverently while you listen to the beautiful music."

This was the cue for the music to come up, and the hall was filled with the lilting strains of yet another arrangement of Johann Pachelbel's famous canon.

"It's too bad he's not getting royalties from that piece," I said. "Too bad *I'm* not getting royalties from that piece."

"Hush," Meg hissed under her breath, giving me an elbow in the side.

"After supper," Jelly continued, "you are invited to go to the sanctuary for a time of meditation and a short sermon by Father Barna."

"Are you going for the sermon?"

"I am not," I said. "I have to prepare for choir practice."

"You never prepare for choir practice," said Meg. "But I'll be happy to help you."

From a distance the entire representation looked quite attractive. But, as the buffet line moved closer to the table, it became apparent that most of the mannequins playing the disciples had seen better days. By the time we had reached the table, several beards were askew and St. Andrew's arm had fallen off, landing in a plate of creamed corn.

Cynthia Johnsson, now back at work at the Ginger Cat, had brought the coffee and was serving it at the Mary Magdalene Coffee Bar. She was, of course, dressed accordingly. I stopped to say hello.

"Cynthia, it's so good to see you. I must say that you look lovely this evening. Sort of like an Arabian hooker."

"I'm Mary Magdalene. I looked her up and found out that she was a prostitute, so I went down and got a belly dancer's outfit in Boone. Do you like it?" She snapped her fingers and did a little spin.

"It's *very* nice. I especially like the bells. I have just two questions. Number one: will you be dancing later? And number two: can Meg borrow the outfit when you're finished?"

"Number one: if the price is right," laughed Cynthia. "And number two: absolutely..."

"NOT!" added Meg, dragging me toward the buffet.

Each mannequin at the table was wearing a beard and dressed in a cloak and a tunic – a nametag affixed to each outfit, presumably so that we could tell one disciple from another. Unfortunately, I wasn't expecting to see nametags at the Last

Supper, and the "Hi, I'm Judas!" badge made me laugh out loud, costing me another dig in the ribs, this time courtesy of Rhiza.

Jelly's plan was for all of the guests to pick up a plate, walk by the tableau, and help themselves to whatever traditional Passover foods they wished to eat. The platters, heaped with food, were placed in front of Jesus and the disciples along with serving utensils. Brenda – dressed as Martha – and Wynette Winslow – dressed as Mary – were going between the tableau and the kitchen, refilling the empty plates. There were a couple of folks in the kitchen as well, dishing up the food. Every few minutes Brenda would stop to glare at Mary Magdalene.

"It looks as though Brenda doesn't appreciate Cynthia's outfit," I said with a grin.

"I'm not sure *I* do either," said Meg with a sniff as we moved through the line.

"I didn't know that St. Matthew was fond of chili enchiladas," I said, pointing them out as I took a helping of Wendy Bolling's baked beans from the plate of James the Less. "I love these beans though."

Suddenly Wynette, obviously tired of running back and forth to the kitchen, decided to yell out her order. "St. Thaddeus is out of stuffed mushrooms! And Bartholomew needs some more cheese grits!"

"Try some of *my* dish," said Mattie Lou Entriken who was two places in front of me. She pointed toward St. Philip who, in turn, was pointing accusingly to a steaming plate of shrimp pasta.

"Shrimp pasta?" I asked.

"I was supposed to bring some matzah ball soup, but since it's a potluck, I wanted to bring something a little tastier. I didn't want to be the only one bringing a lousy dish," Mattie Lou shrugged. "It looks like everyone else had the same idea."

"I'm sure St. Philip would approve of the sentiment, if not the shellfish," I said, taking a helping.

We went through the line and sampled Simon's bread pudding with rum sauce. Matthew's enchiladas were complimented nicely by a delicious chickpea and artichoke salad. Mouth-watering grilled bratwurst and sauerkraut appeared courtesy of Doubting Thomas. Peter, true to his later theological leanings, was serving bacon-wrapped pork chops. Andrew had traded creamed corn for asparagus while James and John, the Sons of Thunder, teamed up with barbequed ribs and tuna casserole. Judas was looking dourly at Meg's horseradish sauce and a platter of overcooked lamb with mint jelly that wasn't moving too quickly. Jesus presided over a basket of cornbread and hush-puppies.

I filled my plate and moved to the Mary Magdalene Coffee Bar.

"Don't spend too much time over there," warned Meg. "I notice that the line is all male."

"It's just that we men like our coffee served a certain way."

"By a woman in a skimpy belly-dancer's outfit?"

"Come to think of it, yes. Yes, that's it exactly."

"St. Thomas needs some more brats and kraut," came the call. "And Jesus needs a refill."

"Now there's a line you don't hear too often at a Seder Supper," I said to Meg.

"Here's the processional for Sunday," I said, handing out a hastily scribbled and copied piece of music to the choir. "You'll be walking just in front of the donkey."

The choir had already heard about the donkey. It was the foremost subject of conversation at supper.

"It's a short refrain for the choir with some solos on the verses," I said, as the choir looked over their music. "With a few added handbells for effect, it should be quite lovely. Memorize the refrain. It's only four measures long."

"Are all the children processing as well?" asked Rebecca.

"They are. But they'll be behind the donkey. You guys come in right after Wenceslas. No wait – that's not right. Here's the order. Crucifer, verger, acolytes, thurifer, choir, the donkey with His Eminence astride, the Barnacles, then the children waving the palm branches," I said, counting them off. The Barnacles was the title given to Father Barna's cope attendants by the choir, much to their embarrassment.

"What else are we singing?" asked Fred.

"Victoria's *Hosanna Filio David*, as the introit. Then we'll sing the Casals' *O Vos Omnes* at communion. We have a lot to sing next week. The service on Maundy Thursday at seven. The Good Friday service is at noon for all the men that can be here.

"Hey!" said Marjorie, coming up the stairs, a little late as usual. "Did you hear they found another snake?"

"Where was it?" asked Georgia.

"You won't believe this! It was curled up in Father Barna's spare toupee – the one he keeps in the sacristy! He picked it up to shake it and the snake came slithering out! I'd have given a hundred dollars to see that."

Her merriment was contagious and soon the entire choir was laughing.

"Listen Hayden," said Bev. "Before we get into all this depressing music and," she said smiling, "since we just had that simply stunning reenactment of the authentic last supper, may we please sing through *The Weasel Cantata*? There are several new choir members who haven't sung it."

"I've never sung it," quipped Rebecca. "We were going to sing it last Christmas when I joined the choir, but we never did."

"I haven't sung it either," added Christina. Several others nodded their heads.

"Fine," I said, looking over the balcony rail and seeing Father Barna deep in conversation with Jelly and Princess Foo-Foo. "This may be just the right time to go through it."

The choir members had *The Weasel Cantata*[2] stashed in the back of their folders along with several other repugnant pieces I had written over the years including a motet entitled *Like As The Dog Returns From His Vomit* (on Proverbs 26:11). *The Weasel Cantata*, however, had the distinction of being the only piece ever written on the dietary laws of Leviticus and takes advantage of the fact that the word "weasel" is only mentioned in the Bible one time. Leviticus 11:29 – "And these are unclean to you among the swarming things that swarm upon the earth: the weasel, the mouse, the great lizard according to its kind." The verses flow over a Baroque rendering of *Pop Goes The Weasel* while the choruses are sung to the Thanksgiving hymn *We Gather Together*. It is an altogether lovely and well-crafted work of surpassing beauty. Or so I've been told.

I began the introduction, glancing toward the priestly convocation to make sure they were within earshot.

> *How many times does the weasel appear*
> *In the Bible? just once – and it's perfectly clear,*
> *That Moses and weasels did not get along,*
> *And it's in his mem'ry we're singing this song.*
> *Of all of the animals sitting around*
> *In the Old Testament there may be found*
> *Only one reference to our sly friend*
> *From Genesis 1:1 straight through to the end.*

The choir sang with gusto as they finished the first verse and launched into the Thanksgiving hymn:

[2] Download *The Weasel Cantata* at sjmp.com/pdfs/n.weasel.pdf

The Weasel Cantata, it's not a sonata,
You cannot eat weasel though it may taste fine,
Or lizards or vermin, cause they commence to squirmin'
Leviticus: eleven, verse twenty-nine.

I snuck a peek down at the unholy trinity as we began the second verse. On this verse, the basses all had a little countermelody – *Pop Goes The Weasel* – sung in Latin. Father Barna, Jelly and the Princess were all looking up in disgust.

You can eat all you want of a sheep, but no pork,
And you cannot eat pelican, heron or stork,
Or tortoise or eagles or bugs on the floor,
And if you eat ravens, you'll cry "Nevermore!"
But all of these rules will come down in a trice,
When you develop a taste for fried mice.
For nothing's as tasty, no matter the cost,
As freshly baked mole-pie with iguana sauce!

So if you love weasel, just give it a squeezel,
And don't mind the greasel and it may taste fine,
With lizards and vermin, and never mind the squirmin',
Leviticus: eleven, verse twenty-nine.

The choir finished with aplomb and cheered themselves as they finished. I looked over the balcony rail, but the church was empty.

"OK," I said with a laugh. "Enough of this foolishness. Let's get to work."

I went by the McCollough's trailer on Saturday morning. I had called Ardine on my way up the mountain and she was waiting for me on the makeshift porch. Moosey was behind her, trying to get by, but she had him pinned inside the door.

"Will you quit it!" she admonished. "You can go out in a second."

"I need to talk to you anyway, Moosey," I said as I went up the steps. "I have a job for you."

"How 'bout a candy bar?" Moosey said as he squeezed past his mother and went to my jacket pocket. I raised my hands as he frisked me and found the Milky Way. Then, quicker than Ardine could say "don't spoil your dinner," he had it peeled and half stuffed into his mouth.

"C'mon in," said Ardine, holding the door open. "I just can't teach that boy no manners."

"It's OK. He'll learn them once we send him off to *military school.*" I looked hard at Moosey, but he'd heard the threat before and wasn't fazed by it.

"I wanna go, I tell ya! PLEASE send me to military school!"

"Well, you can't go. Not until you learn some manners," said Ardine, taking the opposite tact. Then she shook her head with a smile. These threats weren't exactly working out as she'd hoped.

I stepped into the living room. The McCollough trailer wasn't fancy, but it was always neat as a pin. Carrying a book, Bud came out of his room at the commotion and stood in the hallway.

"Hello, sir," he said, closing the book with his thumb inside to mark the place. Bud was a voracious reader and the single biggest patron of the St. Germaine library. To suppliment his habit, I brought him a book every week that he dutifully returned once he was finished reading it. He was also St. Germain's foremost authority on fine wines.

151

"Hey Mom," Bud said. "Pauli said to tell you that she was down at Lisa's doing a project. She'll be home before dinner."

"Thank you, Bud."

"Listen Bud," I said. "Anything new on the wine front I should know about?"

"The next time you're in Asheville, go to the Wine Market on Biltmore Avenue and get some *Beringer Gamay Nouvea.* It's based on the same Gamay grape as *Beaulolais Nouveau* but fruitier and simpler. I think you and Miss Farthing will really like it."

"Thanks," I said, writing the information in my notepad. "Oh, by the way, here's an interesting read." I pulled a worn copy of the first of the Horatio Hornblower novels by C.F. Forrester out of my coat pocket.

"Wow!" he said, his eyes lighting up. "I've been wanting to read these, but our library doesn't have them. I was going to try inter-library loan, but I haven't gotten around to it yet."

"Well, I have them all, so don't bother trying to hunt them down."

"That's great!" he said, turning and walking down the hall before throwing a "Thanks!" back over his shoulder.

"OK, Moosey," I said, turning my attention to the real reason I came by. "Here's the thing. We need someone to lead the donkey down the aisle on Sunday morning."

"What donkey?" asked Ardine.

"The donkey for Palm Sunday. Geez, Mom," said Moosey with the disgust evident in his voice that only a six-year old can muster. "Don't you know about anything about religion?"

Ardine looked at me questioningly.

"I'm afraid he's right. The priest is riding a donkey into church on Palm Sunday morning."

"But why?" asked Ardine, finally voicing the question we'd

all been asking ourselves.

"It's hard to say exactly," I said, raising an eyebrow in Moosey's direction. "I'll tell you later. Anyway, we need someone who is good with animals to lead the donkey in. It wouldn't do for Jeremiah to get scared."

"I can do it!" said Moosey. "Sure I can! I've already been over to Connie Ray's about a hundred times to play with him."

"I know you have."

"I told you to leave Connie Ray's animals alone," said Ardine sternly.

"Aw, Mom. He says I can come over and help him any time."

"It's true," I said, sticking up for Moosey. "That's what Connie Ray told me, too. Anytime he wants. And Connie Ray said that Moosey's mighty good with that donkey."

We both looked at Ardine and waited hopefully for her answer.

"All right then," she said, shaking her head. "But don't you two cause any trouble at that church."

Moosey and I looked at each other, then back to Ardine, shook our heads at the same time and answered in unison. "No ma'am. We won't."

"You'll need to bring something for Jeremiah to munch on," I said to Moosey as he and I walked down the steps to my car. "Sometimes donkeys like a little treat. Carrots would be good."

Moosey nodded.

Chapter 15

Chapter 15

I leaned back in my chair and contemplated my next move. The clowns were a problem. Rocki was a problem. Lilith was a problem. The bishop was always a problem. I had more problems than a Viagra sales- man at a Castrati Convention.

The door slammed open and there was another prob- lem. A big problem. It was Race. Race Rankle.

"What are you trying to do?"

"Calm down, Race," I said. "Take off your coat and have a drink."

"Listen, Bub! I don't have time for this, so I'll cut to the bottom line. You help me out and when this merger goes through General Convention, I'll cut you in for two percent."

"What about the clowns?" I asked.

"What clowns? I don't know nothing about no clowns. I've got this leper colony deal workin'."

I'd never had an interest in a leper colony, but I wasn't above taking one. I opened the bottle of Scotch on my desk and poured a couple of fingers into two glasses. Then I took Lilith's fingers out of the glasses and dropped in a couple of cubes. "That Lilith," I thought. "Always leaving trinkets around."

"I'll take fifteen percent of the total," I said, grinning like it was Tuesday and I was the Pope.

"Four percent of the net," came Rankle's reply as he settled into the chair and picked up his glass.

"Twelve percent of the gross," I said, reaching for my drink as well.

"Six and a half--off the top."

"Nine and a quarter--under the table."

"Seven even--down and dirty."

Done," I said.

"Done," said Race, smiling. He lifted his glass to his lips and threw the hooch back like a bad prom date to seal the deal. Then he coughed once and stared at me, his mouth a gaping black hole, opening and closing, like a bass in a fish tank or a bass who forgot the words of the opening hymn, before falling out of the chair. He was dead. As dead as Connie Chung's career. And this was going to be the biggest frame-up since the Energizer Bunny was charged with battery.

Palm Sunday morning dawned bright and cool with blue skies. It was fine weather for a donkey ride, and I intended to arrive at the church in plenty of time to make sure everyone knew what they were doing. I had spoken to Meg on the phone the night before, and she informed me that according to the FOOSCHWAG, the monkey was no longer in his house. Now the pig was in charge, and we mustn't offend the snake.

"Everything is turned around again, but I think there's enough room for the donkey. The chi will be flowing North-Northwest, so try to stay out of the way."

"I'll do my best," I said. "Is the pig really in charge?"

"More than ever! And don't forget. Whatever you do, please avoid offending the snake."

"If I see any more snakes, I won't offend them. Did they get the fountain fixed?"

"Oh, yes. It trickles very nicely now. But I suspect there will be even more trips to the bathroom during the service."

"I expect there will be."

"The pig's earth-sign is water, by the way. And the snake's is fire. It's a very dangerous combination. That's what Mr. Christopher says."

"I'll be careful. See you tomorrow morning."

I would have made it to church with ninety minutes or so to spare – plenty of time to get everyone lined up and in order. I would have, that is, if I hadn't come upon an accident on the highway into town. A car had missed a curve, driven off the road into a ditch and hit a small tree. The driver wasn't hurt, but, being a police officer, I had to write up the accident and give the driver a ride into town where he could call a tow truck. By the time I arrived at St. Barnabas, I had about five minutes to spare before the service started.

"Hayden!" called Princess Foo-Foo as she ran up to meet me. "Thank God you made it! All the children have their palm branches and have lined up behind the donkey. Is that right?'

"It's exactly right, Brenda. Crucifer, verger, acolytes, thurifer, choir, donkey, the Barnacles, then the children."

"I think we're all set then," she said smiling in relief.

"How's Moosey doing?"

"He's doing great. That donkey just loves him and follows him everywhere." Foo-Foo pointed to the front of the pack. I could see a tail whipping back and forth.

"Moosey," I called, making my way to the top of the procession. "How's Jeremiah?"

"Great! I gave him some food just like you said."

"What's that in your hand?"

"What I been feeding him. It's called 'sparagus. He loves it."

I looked on in horror as Jeremiah ate the last spear. "Where did you get asparagus?"

"In the church kitchen. I left my carrots at home. This was

left over in the fridge from that dinner."

"Did you feed him anything else?" I asked, dread now evident in my voice. I was reasonably certain that I had seen the only other leftovers from the *Edible Last Supper*.

"About four of them chili enchiladas."

In retrospect, I think we all felt the sorriest for the Barnacles since they were directly *behind* the donkey carrying Father Barna's train. A donkey's digestive system is not set up for asparagus and chili enchiladas, no matter how he may enjoy eating them.

The procession began with the handbells ringing, the organ playing and the choral refrain of "Lift up your heads, ye mighty gates; behold the King of glory waits" echoing through the sanctuary. True to Meg's description, the altar was now set up in the north to take advantage of the pig's energy. This was, to some degree, more like our usual setup, and at least not as totally foreign as when the monkey was in his house. I much preferred the pig.

The crucifer came in followed by Wenceslas, resplendent in his velvet tam and cloak, goose-stepping along behind the cross. Behind Wenceslas were the acolytes and then Benny Dawkins, our champion thurifer, who was swinging the smoking incense pot and going through his bag of tricks quite nicely. He presented the "Three-Leaf Clover," the "Over the Falls," and his special "Rock the Baby," before finally finishing up with his trademark swing that had earned him the Bronze Medal at the International Thurifer Invitational in London – the "Doubly-Inverted Reverse Swan."

The choir was next, singing the refrain when it came around, and deferring to the soloists, Bev and Bob, for the remainder of the piece.

Moosey and the donkey were behind the choir. Moosey was

leading Jeremiah by a rope tied to his halter while Father Barna sat on the beast of burden's back and waved to the congregation like the Rose Bowl Queen on New Year's Day. Father Barna's attendants – the Barnacles – were following him, directly behind Jeremiah, carrying the train of the priest's cope. Walking behind the donkey were about thirty children and a few parents. They all had palm branches in their hands and were waving then frenetically – occasionally sticking a palm into the eye of an unwary parishioner foolish enough to have claimed an aisle seat on Palm Sunday. All told, it was quite a scene they made as they paraded into the church from the front steps.

The donkey made it about half way down the aisle before the first explosion happened. I call it an explosion because the phrase "a little donkey gas" would not begin to describe the breathtaking volume of the sound followed by the unfathomable odor that arose to the choir loft like a stench from the depths of hell.

"Oh my God!" muttered Beverly, quickly pulling her choir robe up around her mouth and nose. To his everlasting credit, Bob, who had just started singing, gagged only once before choking out the rest of his solo. The choir didn't do as well, spinning around to see what had transpired, their eyes wide with disbelief. Several of them made it to the choir loft, Megan included, before the next refrain came around. It didn't help. None of them could utter a sound.

The second explosion sent all the children running for cover, palm fronds thrown to the wind. The Barnacles didn't know what to do. They were directly in harm's way but were holding Father Barna's cope and didn't dare let go. Finally, Randy, the younger of the two, covered his mouth and ran from the building. Lester wasn't far behind.

With a huge "HEE-HAW" from Jeremiah – a cry of anguish if ever a donkey has uttered one – another explosion occurred, this one more powerful than the two that had come before. I stopped playing. The chili enchiladas and asparagus were proving to be a deadly combination. With another bray, Jeremiah sat down in the middle of the aisle and refused to move. The congregation had begun to move toward the exits, first as unobtrusively as possible, but then, as the smell overcame them, in a headlong dash. Wenceslas and Moosey had disappeared into the sacristy with the acolytes in tow. Father Barna had slid down Jeremiah's back and was trying to pull the ends of his cope from underneath the donkey's hindquarters. It was no use. He was trapped.

The choir was silent as we all viewed the next event with reverent awe.

Jeremiah gave a low groan. Then with a series of very fast "HAW-HAW-HAW-HAWs" he lept to his feet. Father Barna, his cope coming free, fell backward directly behind the donkey. We all watched in wonder, our robes protecting our noses, as Jeremiah's tail came up and he gave one last anguished bray.

"HEEEE-HAAAW!"

It was then that Father Emil Barna, "God's Voice in Appalachia," received again the sacrament of baptism, this time by immersion.

"Oh dear Lord God, blessed be your Holy Name," Georgia muttered with a smile.

"Who's going to clean that up?" asked Christina.

"We'll have to call a cleaning service," Meg said. "Unbelievable! I didn't know a donkey could do that. It's like that time the hose came loose on Jeffrey Hine's truck when he was vacuuming out those portable toilets."

"It was the enchiladas," I explained through the cassock covering my mouth. "That, plus the asparagus."

I looked back down at the carnage. Jeremiah, feeling much better, was heading toward the front door. Father Barna was rolling on the floor, calling for help.

"I think that the Palm Sunday service has ended," I said. "Go in peace to love and serve the Lord."

Chapter 16

"I'm really not responsible for that," I told Meg. Our appetites had returned by supper, and we were having grilled cheese sandwiches and a new black and tan ale I had found, called *Mississippi Mud.*

"This is good beer," Meg said, taking a sip. "And you are definitely responsible. I don't know how exactly, but you are."

"I told Moosey to give the donkey some carrots. You know, to lead him down the aisle. Not asparagus and chili enchiladas."

"Well, Ardine was sure mad. I can tell you that! She said that you and Moosey promised there'd be no trouble."

"Well, how do you think I feel? All that work that the choir did preparing those pieces is down the drain. We can use the Victoria piece after Easter, but we can't sing *O Vos Omnes* until next year."

"If they have the church cleaned up by then."

"I think that the FOOSCHWAG must have offended the pig," I said. "It sure smelled worse than a sty in there."

"Very funny. Billy Hixon says he can get a cleaning crew in there tonight to start work. He says that it'll cost twice as much, but if they wait until tomorrow, it may be too late."

"On the up side, there may not be very much support for Father Barna's application to serve as permanent rector."

"You're probably right there. Although, if the vestry thinks that you had anything to do with it, you may be the one out of a job."

"I am innocent of all charges. I have been nothing but supportive to Father Barna, Jelly, Princess Foo-Foo, Wenceslas, Mr. Christopher and all their cronies."

"That's sort of true. The snakes, of course, were your fault."

"Not mine. Those snakes escaped on their own."

163

"You brought the snake handler in."

"Father Barna asked me to."

"Really?" Meg asked doubtfully.

"That's my story and I'm stickin' to it."

"Spring at last," said Pete Moss as I walked into the Slab for our Monday morning staff meeting. "It's supposed to get up into the sixties today."

Nancy was drinking coffee at the table and waiting for her breakfast. Dave hadn't shown up yet.

"I guess it's time," I said. "Gardens are supposed to go in by Good Friday."

"They're going to be late this year," said Nancy. "No one in their right mind would put in a garden for at least a month."

"You'd be surprised," I said. "Old timers swear by the Almanac." I turned my attention to the kitchen. "Hey, Noylene! Do you think I can get a haircut this afternoon?"

Noylene stuck her head out of the swinging door. "Can you come by around two?"

"I'll be here."

Nancy pulled her pad out of her pocket and set it on the table. It was now official – our meeting had begun. With or without Dave.

"How's your hand?" asked Nancy, trying to look at the small scar that remained on my palm.

"Good as new," I said, holding up my hand for her to see. "That Dermabond is amazing stuff. No stitches!"

"Just like superglue," said Nancy. "Anything new on the clown case?"

"We don't even know if it *is* a case. Unless we can prove foul play, I guess it'll be ruled an accident."

Nancy nodded. "Did you ever get any information back from

the Chapel Hill police?"

"Not yet. We can't even find a next-of-kin."

I called Hugh when I got back to the office. It was about two in the afternoon, England time, and he picked up on the third ring.

"Glad I caught you," I said. "I think I have it figured out. At least part of it. I should have thought of it before, but I was so sure the diamond was in the water."

"Well, you can't be right *all* the time."

"Sure I can. Anyway, one of the men you're looking for is the policeman whose daughter was singing a solo in the choir. I'm pretty sure he's involved – if not in the murder, then certainly in the theft."

"That would be Alex Benwick. But he's been with the Minster force for three or four years."

"Any problems at home?"

"He got divorced last summer. The missus ended up with the two children. It hasn't been an easy situation for him. I only know because I was counseling with him."

"I think the police should check him out. And maybe search his house."

"Why do you think it was him?"

"A few reasons. Number one. He was conveniently out of the office when the cameras were turned off. Number two. He had access to a key and could have easily given it to Kris. Number three. His daughter was singing the soprano solo in the Stanford *Magnificat.* That's the opening solo. She would have been finished by 5:15 at the latest, but he didn't return to the office until after evensong was over thirty minutes later. Number four – and this is what I should have caught earlier. I'm betting that the fake diamond was set back into the chalice using Dermabond."

165

"The surgical glue they used to stick your hand back together after you cut it?"

"The very stuff. They had a couple of small tubes of it in the Minster Police's first-aid kit. You can check it against the glue on the back of the CZ. I'll bet that the chemical makeup is the same."

"But why would he do it?"

"I don't know. Could be a lot of reasons, but he most probably did it for the money. Check on his debt to salary ratio if you can. If you do a little digging, it won't be hard to find the reason why."

"I'll alert the Minster Police and give you a call back if they find anything."

"Great! Talk to you soon."

"Now I've got you, flatfoot."

I knew it would come to this as soon as I called the coppers, but I could see no way around it. Race was dead. Mackerel dead. Doornail dead. Abraham Lincoln dead. And he was in my office, a poisoned drink on his lips.

"Take it easy, Lieutenant. You know I'm not good for it. I'm the one who called it in."

"Looks to me like you're the main suspect." He pointed to the dead body. "An acquaintance of yours?"

"Never seen him before."

"Yea, sure. Then how is it that he's dead on your floor after drinking your booze? And why is he wearing an evening gown?"

That caught me by surprise. Race's trench coat had fallen open when he hit the floor. I looked again. A Versace knock-off. Not bad, I thought. Probably paid about three-hundred for it. It was strapless--a Basque waist with a straight cut bust line in a champagne floral print. Size 28.

"So, what can you tell me? Do you know him? Is this some kind of chintz?"

"Yea, I know him," I said. "He's a baritone. And it's chiffon."

"At last," said Meg, skimming the page hanging half out of the typewriter. "At last we get to it. I wondered how long it would take you. The baritone wore chiffon. Another cross-dressing moment in detective literature."

I was grilling a couple of steaks in the kitchen and tossing Archimedes a mouse every once in a while. He was sitting in the window propping it open, and he seemed to be especially hungry this evening. While the steaks were sizzling, I rummaged around my bookshelf and found my favorite recording of Handel's *Messiah* recorded by St. Martin's in the Field. It was Holy Week, after all, and I planned to listen to all three hours of it tonight.

"You'll be glad to know," I called out, "that I'm pretty sure that I'll be finishing it up soon. Lent is almost over."

"We're all very relieved to hear it," Meg said as she came into the kitchen. My *Messiah*-thon had started, and the overture was echoing through the house.

"Are the interviews still on?" I asked.

"The first candidate – the man – is coming on the Friday after Easter. He'll interview, meet the vestry and then preach the next Sunday morning. Father Barna wouldn't let him celebrate communion."

"That figures."

"The woman will be here the week after that. Same schedule. She may be celebrating because Father Barna is scheduled to be gone. He might change his mind though and stick around."

I took the baked potatoes out of the oven, gave the salad a final toss, and helped Meg dish up the food.

"When are we going to start our Sunday after-church picnicking again?"

"How about after the last priestly candidate is here? I'd sort of like to be around for those," I said.

"That sounds like a plan."

We were just starting to eat when the phone rang. It was Hugh.

"A little late where you are, isn't it?" I said.

"About one in the morning."

"What did you find out?"

"Alex Benwick – you know – the Minster Policeman with the daughter – hasn't been into work for three days. He called in the first day and said he was ill. He didn't call in the second two days, but everyone assumed he was still feeling under the weather."

"Did you go by his house?"

"The Minster Police got in touch with the Yorkshire Police and went to his flat. I went with them, of course."

"Of course."

"He was there, all right. Drunk as a lord. Had been for days, I reckon. He was read his rights and he just started crying. Blurted out the whole story even though the police tried to shut him up. They thought that since he was drunk, his confession might not stand up in court. He wouldn't stop, though. Just kept sobbing the story out."

"Let's hear it then."

"He'd been up to his neck in gambling. It's why his wife left him in the first place. I couldn't tell you that the first time we talked. It was confidential."

"I understand."

"He got in trouble with some very bad people and he needed some money in a hurry. Then one night after services, he got to talking with Kris Toth over a pint down at the Golden Fleece. It seems that Kris had a plan to steal something out of the treasury. All Alex had to do was make sure the cameras were off and get Kris a key to one of the cabinets. Kris would take care of everything else. She'd steal the diamond – although, at that point, Alex wasn't told what would be stolen – replace the diamond with a fake and return the key to Alex. No one would be the wiser. The theft might not have been discovered for years."

"What was in it for Alex?"

"Kris told him that he'd get fifty thousand pounds once the diamond was sold."

"Let me guess what happened next," I said. "Alex got greedy, went down to the treasury, they had a scuffle for the diamond and Alex killed her."

"Not according to Alex. He says he didn't go into the treasury at all. Not until Kris was found dead. He says that Kris came to him in a panic right before Evensong that night and asked for some glue. Apparently she'd forgotten to get any. All that Alex had was the Dermabond in the first-aid kit, so he gave Kris a tube. The next time he saw Kris, she was dead on the floor."

"Did he know that Kris was a woman?"

"He says he had no idea."

"Did you search his house for the diamond?"

"He's in custody. They'll search his house tomorrow, but I doubt that they'll find anything. I'm a pretty good judge of confessions – God knows, I've heard enough of them – and this one rings true."

"I think you're probably right. This means that there's someone else involved as well. And I might have an idea who."

"Can you tell me?"

"Not just yet. Let me do a little more sleuthing."

"Are you coming over?"

"Nope. I think I can do it from here."

"Really? This is becoming most curious."

"It's more curious than you think," I said.

Chapter 17

"Dave," I said, as I walked into the office, shed my light coat, and poured a cup of coffee. "Would you get me the Ringling Brothers Circus Museum on the phone?"

"And exactly how would I do that?" asked Dave.

"Call information. I think the place is located in Sarasota."

"I'll give it a try."

I doctored my coffee, got a donut out of a day-old box and made it to my office by the time Dave called out, "Line two."

"Thanks," I said, picking up the receiver. "Is this the Circus Museum? Yes? This is Detective Konig from St. Germaine in North Carolina. I wonder if you have a circus historian at the museum? May I speak with him please?"

There was a short pause. Then a voice seasoned with age came on the line.

"Hello. This is Roger Watkins."

"Mr. Watkins, this is Detective Hayden Konig with the St. Germaine Police Department. I understand that you're the historian for the museum and I wonder if you can help me. I'm working on a murder investigation."

"Yes, Detective. I'll certainly help if I can."

"I'm looking for some information on an old circus family. The family would have been active in Europe at the end of the last century."

"Just a moment and I'll pull up our data base."

I waited a minute and the voice came back on the line.

"I have it now. What's the family you're looking for?"

"The name is Kaszas. Hungarian. Probably from Budapest."

"Ah, the Kaszas family. I won't even have to look that one up. Der Kaszas Kaiserlicher Zirkus. Or if you prefer – The Kaszas Imperial Circus."

"German?"

"Austrian actually. But in the late nineteenth century, it was an Austro-Hungarian empire. The circus was, in fact, based in Budapest but they were a favorite of Emperor Franz Josef and so spent most of their time in Vienna. They were a very famous troupe, playing everywhere from England to Russia and as far north as Sweden. All over Europe actually."

"What happened to them? Are they still around?"

"Well, presumably the descendants are. Hang on a second and I'll pull the history up. My memory isn't what it used to be. Yes, there it is."

"The Kaiserlicher Zirkus had its last official performance in 1918 at the end of the World War I. It was scheduled to play in St. Petersburg, Russia, but ended up going to Yekaterinburg, several days journey to the south. They traveled by train, of course."

"Do the records indicate which month?" I asked.

"No, but it would have been late spring or summer. The circus didn't perform in the winter."

"Yekaterinburg? That's incredible!"

"Yes. It would have been a dangerous trip."

"Is there anything else?"

"The circus disbanded because their train couldn't make it back. It was confiscated by the Bolsheviks and never returned. The circus went bankrupt. The performers that did manage to get back to Budapest joined other shows after the war. Several joined the Forepaugh-Sells Show. Others came over to America and joined P.T. Barnum."

"Wow! Can you do another search for me?"

"Surely."

"Are there any entries for a bareback rider named Howes? A woman."

"Just a second." I waited for a moment, still trying to make sense of what I was hearing.

"There are many Howes listed but only one bareback rider. Belle Howes. Second wife of Seth B. Howes. Seth was just about the wealthiest circus owner in the business in the 1870's. Next to P.T. Barnum, that is. In the 1850s, the Howes Circus included 'the Celebrated and Original General Tom Thumb.' Seth sold the entire enterprise to James Bailey in 1870 who in turn united the show with P.T. Barnum in 1880. The Howes name was dropped when the circus became Barnum and Bailey's 'Greatest Show on Earth.' Madam Howes came to America long before 1918 though. I show that she was a featured bareback rider in 1868. 'The Incomparable Madam Howes.' She was called 'Madam' because she was married, but she was probably around eighteen years old or so."

"Do you show Belle Howes' maiden name?" I asked.

"Why, yes I do."

"And it is...?"

"Kaszas."

I met with Meg at the Slab for lunch and invited Nancy to come along, leaving Dave to mind the store. Business was picking up around town, now that the weather had turned, and the café had more than its usual customers. All around town shopkeepers were sprucing up their storefronts, moving displays out onto the sidewalks and cleaning the salt and mud splatters off their windows. Looking up into the hardwoods, I could make out just a hint of green. Another few days and the leaves would open, changing the look of St. Germaine completely. It would happen, seemingly, overnight and, although I preferred cold weather, it was always a pleasure to watch another spring break forth.

"A Reuben sandwich for me, Noylene," I said, sitting down and not bothering to look at the menu. "And a Coke." I had taken a booth in the back rather than our usual up-front table.

"Meg said to order her a club platter and a water. Nancy can order when she gets here."

"I'll get it started," said Noylene. "Oh, wait. Here they are now."

Nancy and Meg came in the door and walked back to the booth.

"This is pretty secretive," said Nancy. "We hardly ever use a booth." She turned to Noylene. "I'll have the Turkey Blue-Plate Special."

"Did you order for me?" asked Meg, sliding in.

"Club sandwich platter and a water," said Noylene.

"I'll have iced tea," said Nancy. Noylene noted it in her pad, nodded and walked back to the kitchen.

"Why the meeting?" Nancy said.

"I need to lay this all out. Meg is up on the England case," I said, "and you're up on the Peppermint case. And here's the thing." I looked at Meg, then at Nancy. "They're related."

"How can they be?" asked Meg.

"I don't know how, yet. I just know that they are. Here's what I know about the York case."

"Kris Toth, studying on a fellowship and with a position as a baritone in the Minster choir, was strangled after having been knocked unconscious. It turned out that Kris, although the proud owner of a pretty convincing beard and a good baritone voice, was a she. She was strangled in the treasury of the Minster with her own black panty-hose."

"The autopsy revealed that Kris Toth suffered from hirsutism. That is, excessive hair growth. The condition runs in families and, in her case, was caused by abnormally high levels of androgens. She could have controlled it with medication, but apparently chose not to."

"She was found dead in the middle of the Roman ruins, wearing a Victoria's Secret outfit underneath her choir robe and clutching a cross. This cross was thought to have been worn by Czar Nicholas II when he was assassinated. If the story were true it would be a valuable piece, but its value is miniscule when compared to the diamond – worth 1.3 million pounds, by the way – that was taken and replaced with a 32-carat cubic zirconium. The CZ had been set into the chalice using Dermabond, an adhesive similar to Superglue but with medical applications. We presumed that an accomplice killed her, but her only accomplice has already been apprehended. Alex Benwick, a Minster Policeman, had some bad gambling debts. When Kris offered him the opportunity to rid himself of the debts with very little risk, he took it. All he had to do was turn the cameras off, give Kris the key to the cabinet and stay out of the way for forty minutes. He did exactly that and, although he's still a suspect, he doesn't have the diamond, and I don't think he killed her."

I paused to make sure the two women were following everything. "Any questions so far?"

Nancy was taking notes as fast as she could. Meg just shook her head and I could tell by her intent gaze that she was still with me.

"Here's where it gets interesting," I said with a wolfish grin. "You remember that article that Pete put in the paper? St. Germaine Cop called to help in English murder investigation?"

They both nodded.

"It was picked up by the AP and appeared in several statewide papers. The next thing we knew, we had a new priest."

"Huh?" said Nancy. "What has that got to do with anything?"

"Bear with me. It gets complicated. I need to go back to the cabinet in the treasury of York Minster."

"There were several items in the cabinet, but two important

ones. The first is, of course, the missing diamond. A woman named Mrs. Howes left it to the Minster in 1927. Her friend, Lily Forepaugh, delivered the diamond and informed the Minster that she was carrying out Mrs. Howes' last request. The diamond and the offer of a chalice to set it in were accepted gratefully, although no reason for the gift was ever given. The second important item is the cross that Kris was clutching in her hand. At the time, we couldn't figure out why she had taken the cross. It didn't make any sense."

"I'm jumping ahead now," I said. "Back to our interim priest."

"We've got it so far," said Megan. Nancy nodded her affirmation.

"Emil Barna was assigned by the bishop and very quickly if you recall."

"I remember it was a shock to all of us. We thought Father Tony would be our priest until we had a permanent replacement," Meg said.

"Father Barna appeared, seemingly out of the blue, and with him came his valet, Wenceslas Kaszas, the dwarf. I had a talk with Wenceslas. He's from an old circus family in Budapest, but the family stopped performing after World War I. The name of the circus was Der Kaszas Kaiserlicher Zirkus – the Kaszas Imperial Circus. They were very well known in Europe at the turn of the century."

"Wenceslas came over to America from Hungary about two years ago and took a job as Father Barna's manservant. And here's an interesting tidbit. Emil Barna, Wenceslas, Jelly, and Kris Toth are all Hungarian. Maybe second or third generation, but all from the same region. And Peppermint the Clown, a.k.a. Joseph Meyer? Hungarian, as well."

"Does that mean something?" asked Nancy.

"Glad you asked," I said, as Noylene returned with our food.

"Hang on a second. We don't want this to get cold."

Noylene put our plates and drinks on the table and made an unobtrusive exit.

"OK," said Meg. "Continue please."

"We have to go back to 1918," I said, and took a bite of my Reuben. "Mnmphtn mpht..."

"Don't talk with your mouth full," said Nancy.

"Mmph," I mumbled, swallowing the corned beef and sauerkraut. "Sorry. 1918. The end of the Great War. The Kaszas Imperial Circus was engaged to play St. Petersburg. It was a command performance. But the train was rerouted instead to another city. After the performance, the Bolsheviks commandeer the train and wouldn't let it return to Budapest. The circus, without its wagons or other properties, went bankrupt, and the performers, those that make it out of Russia, found work with other troupes."

"Are you ready?" I asked with a smug smile. Meg and Nancy both nodded.

"The city the train was redirected to...the city where the Kaszas Imperial Circus gave its last performance..." I paused for effect. It was a theatrical moment.

"OK, already!" snapped Nancy.

"It was Yekaterinburg. July, 1918."

"It wasn't!" said Megan, the hushed amazement evident in her voice.

"It was!" I said, feeling self-satisfied by my tale.

"What?" asked Nancy. "What's the deal?"

"I can't believe it!" whispered Meg.

"I know it. It's incredible."

"C'mon!" said Nancy, her frustration evident. "Tell me what's going on!"

"But that means..." started Meg.

"Exactly!" I said.

"Aaaargh!" said Nancy through gritted teeth.

"Listen," I said to Meg. "Nancy's learning to speak Pirate."

"And very well too. She speaks it almost as well as you."

"Aaaargh!" I said, answering the charge in perfect Bucaneese, "me thinks it not so, me hearty." I turned my attention back to Nancy and switched to conventional English. "Here's the thing, Nancy. In July of 1918, Nicholas II, the Czar of Russia, and his entire family were assassinated by the Bolsheviks. They had been sent into exile to a city in the Ural mountains. That city was Yekaterinburg."

"Holy smokes!" said Nancy. "Nicholas and Alexandra? Anastasia? *That* Nicholas II?"

"The very same."

"Then the cross that was in Kris Toth's hand when she was killed must have something to do with all this. But what's the connection?"

I nodded and continued. "Mrs. Howes, who gave the diamond to the Minster..."

Nancy and Meg both looked at me now, waiting for the other shoe to drop.

"...Was a bareback rider for the Howes-Cushing and later, The Barnum and Bailey Circus. She was the second wife of Seth Howes, the owner, but she came to the states long before 1918. Her stage name was Madam Howes. Her maiden name was Belle Kaszas."

Chapter 18

I walked out of the police station and into the
cold night air, the wind playing with my collar like
a cheap floozy at a piano bar. I lit up a stogie,
hoping it would take the chill off. It did. I reviewed
my facts.

There had been a murder. Canon Shannon Cannon had
been killed by a poison collar meant for the bishop.
The bishop wanted me to find out who did it and put
the kibosh on the hit; or so said his personal trainer,
Rocki Pilates, a woman with a lot to hide and not
many clothes to hide it in. She had more angles than
Pythagoras. And there were other players as well.

Lilith Hammerschmidt, professional leper, and her
singing snake, Rolf. Lilith wanted the bishop to put
his stamp on the diocesan merger, a merger that would
guarantee Race Rankle, ex-priest, the money to fund
his leper colony--a boondoggle if ever I heard one.
But now Race was dead and so was Lilith's dream of
becoming the head maid in a high-rise leper-condo
that was permanently unclean.

Uncle Winky, a killer clown with an agenda. The
bishop was bringing a resolution to the convention
dissolving the Ministry of Clowns. But I knew something that Uncle Winky didn't. The bishop was a
Closet-Clown. He'd mimed his way up and down Fourth
Street for years hiding behind a beret, a black and
white striped shirt and enough make-up to clog the
drain in Tammy Faye's gold-plated sink.

And then there was Kit, Girl-Friday; cute in the
way that a Pomeranian was cute when he wasn't treat-

ing your leg like he was a congressman and your leg
was paying the taxes. She'd proved her worth, and I
was going to keep her around.

With the merger quashed, the only problems left
were the clowns. And I'd take care of that.

"Kit!" I called. "It's time to pay a visit to the
circus."

The next morning I borrowed Meg's Lexus and was on my
way to Raleigh to talk to Kris Toth's mother. I could have taken
my old pick-up, but after forty years, it was showing its age. Even
though it was a three-hour drive, I was pretty sure I could make it
there and back before choir rehearsal. I had a long rehearsal
planned. We needed to practice for Maundy Thursday, the Good
Friday service that the men were singing, and our Easter Morning service. As I drove down the mountains, I took pleasure in the
scenery and contemplated which of the yearly services I enjoyed
the most. I found the Maundy Thursday service to be very moving and it was one of my favorites, but Easter morning was probably first on my list, followed by Christmas Eve. Then Maundy
Thursday. Definitely third, I thought.

Four trombones and the organ, a somber and majestic combination, would accompany Thursday's service. The Good Friday
service was chanted unaccompanied by our "Monk's Choir," i.e.
all the men that were available at noon. Our Easter music included
selections from *Messiah* and the traditional Easter hymns of St.
Barnabas, hymns I didn't dare change. For those folks who only
showed up once or twice a year, those hymns were important.

These services had been planned for months – months before Father Barna had arrived – and the vestry had made it clear
to him that he was not to make any changes without their say-so.
I hadn't heard any rumblings, so I was hopeful – although not

entirely convinced.

I traveled the familiar, winding highway and reached I-40 in a little over an hour. Two hours later I was pulling into the driveway of Mrs. Margot Toth.

"Mrs. Toth, I'm so sorry for your loss." I was sitting on a yellow sofa with clear plastic seat covers in the middle of a green shag jungle. It was a scene from the 70s, complete with a Formica kitchen table which originally had been bought for $79.95 including the chairs, but was now probably worth a fortune. Mrs. Toth was a sturdy woman, not much over five feet tall, with black hair tied into a tight bun. She had a no-nonsense look that, coupled with her arched Roman nose and thin, hard lips, gave the impression of a school matron of whom you would *not* wish to run afoul. She was wearing an apron over her plain cotton black dress and was continually drying her hands even though they obviously weren't wet. I had seen grief before, and hers was still fresh.

"You're that man from the newspaper," she said, staring at me intently. Her accent was slightly foreign, but not distracting, the clipped European accent of someone who had lived in America for a long while.

"Yes, ma'am, I am." She had obviously seen the article that had appeared in the paper. "I'm looking into your daughter's death."

She nodded. "I do not know how I can help you. She was very happy to get the scholarship and to be singing with the choir. She sent me a recording."

"I wonder if you know anyone named Kaszas."

She waited a moment, as if judging what I already knew before she answered.

"Yes, I do. Wenceslas Kaszas. We are Hungarian. The community in this area is not large, but it is not small either. We all meet regularly, and we sometimes have services in Magyar at St. Elizabeth's Church. Wenceslas Kaszas would be a hard person to miss."

"Yes, he certainly would. I ask because there may be a connection between Wenceslas and York Minster that I'm trying to piece together."

"I do not know anything," she said very slowly, enunciating each word. With that sentence, her eyes narrowed and her lips grew thinner than I thought possible, almost disappearing altogether. I knew from experience that this part of the interview was over.

"Is Kris buried here in Raleigh?" I asked, changing the subject.

"Yes," Mrs. Toth replied, sadness pervading her voice "Yes, she is."

"Just one more thing. Did they send back Kris's effects? Her belongings?"

"They sent them back with the body. I gave them all to her cousin. She asked to have them. I was just going to throw them away. I do not want any of them here." Her head dropped, and tears ran down her cheeks. She didn't wipe them away. "I am going back to Hungary."

She looked up and nodded toward the fireplace mantle. "That came in the post yesterday," she said, gesturing to an old book with a well-worn leather cover. "The note said that it was her prayerbook."

"May I see it? I collect antique prayerbooks and hymnals."

"You may have it. It is not a prayerbook to me. It is a curse."

I got off the couch, walked over to the mantle and picked up the book. It was a clean copy of the 1662 edition, probably printed in the late eighteenth century and included the Psalms. It was a nice book to have, of course, but wouldn't be usable in a modern service. I had three or four like it back in St. Germaine.

"It will have an honored place in my collection. At least let me pay you for it," I offered, but she waved me off.

"It is part of the curse. This family lives under a curse." She wiped her eyes for the first time with her apron. "If that is all..." she said, indicating that my visit was at an end.

"May I use your bathroom?" I asked. "It's a long trip back."

She nodded and pointed down the hall. "It is the first door on the right."

I walked down the hall, visited the facilities and was washing my hands when I happened to glance at a family picture on the wall above the vanity. Although there were at least twenty people in the photograph, there were a few familiar faces. I looked closer and recognized Margot Toth. Beside her was probably Kris, but I couldn't tell for sure. The face looked the same, but the beard was gone and she was wearing jeans and a sweatshirt. But the easiest face to pick out was Wenceslas. He was standing front and center like the patriarch of a dynasty.

I made a quick side trip to the Chapel Hill police station since I was in the area and chatted with Detective Mike Branson, an old friend of mine.

"Haven't seen you in a while," he said, shaking my hand over his desk. "You skipped the Atlanta conference last month."

"Yeah. Something came up. I couldn't get down there. Was it any good?"

"Mostly more of the same. A good networking opportunity though."

"Wish I could have made it."

"Anyway," he said, "What can I do for you?"

"I called down a few weeks ago about an investigation I was

working on. The vic's name was Joseph Meyers. I wondered if you guys had come up with anything. He was from Chapel Hill, but we couldn't find any next of kin to notify."

"Was it a murder?" Mike asked.

"We don't know for sure. It might have been a series of unfortunate events."

"Let me check. Grab a cup of coffee. I'll be right back."

I poured myself a cup of bad coffee and busied myself reading all of Mike's commendations hanging on the wall. He was back a moment later, followed by a much more attractive officer wearing a uniform.

"Here's the file. Joanie's been collecting the stuff that's come in. She can answer your questions if anyone can." He handed it to me and I sat back down, opening the manila folder and flipping through the pages. Some of these I had already seen.

"Couldn't find a next-of-kin?" I asked.

"Nope," said Joanie. "We went through his house. Nothing. We did find some medical records. They're in the back there. We asked the doctor, but Meyers didn't list anyone to contact in case of emergency. The doctor was a referral from a psychiatrist. We talked to him also. Same result."

"Emphysema," I said, skimming the doctor's report. "We found that."

"It was bad. He also was overweight, had a hole in his lung, a slight heart arrhythmia and was subject to severe panic attacks that totally incapacitated him. An altogether unhealthy fellow. The psychiatrist had prescribed Valium. The medical doc wanted him to cut down on the dosage. Is this any help?"

"I think it is. Did you talk to the psychiatrist?"

"Yep," said Joanie.

"Were these attacks brought on by anything in particular? Crowds? Performing? Did the psychiatrist say anything about stage-fright?"

"All of the above plus some," said Joanie. "The panic attacks didn't show up until a couple of years ago. He didn't have any money that we could locate – no savings accounts, no retirement– so he had to keep working. Here's the kicker. Meyer even developed a fear of clowns, if you can believe that."

"Imagine that." I shook my head. Peppermint had a fear of clowns.

"That wasn't the worst. The worst was ophiciophobia. I remember that one because I have it too. Probably not as bad as he did."

"And that is...?" I asked, looking up from the report.

"The fear of snakes."

I called Dr. Dougherty from my car on my way home later that afternoon.

"Hi Karen. In your role as an esteemed medical professional, could you give me some information?"

"If I can."

"Aldactone," I said. "I hope I'm pronouncing it right."

"You are. It's the brand name for spironolactone. It used to be a drug for high blood pressure, but it's not prescribed much anymore. There may be other applications. Hang on a minute."

Karen came back on a few moments later. "I *thought* I remembered something else. Spironolactone is now mainly prescribed to block testosterone, especially in women. It's quite effective at controlling excessive hair growth – the medical term is hirsutism – but the doses are much higher than for high blood pressure. It's also a diuretic, so you have be careful to drink plenty of water."

"I remember that part. I was taking it for high blood pressure about ten years ago."

"Ever heard of hirsutism?"

"Strangely enough I have. Thanks for your help."

"No problem. I'll talk to you later."

"Wonderful news!" said Georgia, as soon as I showed up at the church. "The FOOSCHWAG has been disbanded! The vestry has decided that Feng Shui is not an appropriate direction for St. Barnabas to be heading in."

"Really? And it only took them six weeks to decide this?"

"Jelly is livid, but tomorrow the movers are coming to return everything to normal."

"No kidding?"

"Pews, altar, paraments...everything," said Georgia, barely able to contain her delight. "And about time, too."

"What about Father Barna's application for the position? Any word on that?"

"Let's just say that his approval rating isn't as high as his opinion of himself."

I was running late the next morning, but managed to answer the phone on the fifth ring as I was coming out of the shower. For the first time all year I hadn't bothered to set my alarm – I never did in the spring and summer, relying instead on Mother Nature to wake me. She had let me down. The weather, a lovely week of early spring sunshine had, overnight, turned miserable. The temperature dropped about twenty degrees, and a storm had come in behind the cold front. It was overcast and raining when I finally awakened, brewed a pot of coffee and jumped into the shower. I came out a few moments later.

"Hello?" I said, trying to tie my robe with one hand and juggle the phone with the other.

"Hayden? It's Lindsey."

"Lindsey. How are you? To what do I owe this pleasant surprise?"

"I'm here in Boone and I thought we could get together."

"You're in Boone? Is there another conference at Appalachian State?"

"No conference. I'd just like to see you."

"You came all this way just to visit?"

"Well, I've been thinking about you quite a bit."

"I must admit, I've been thinking about you, too. Thanks for coming up. I have some work to do up at the church, and then I need to check in at the office. Do you want to meet me there?"

"No. Why don't you come on over to Boone. I'll meet you in the lobby of my hotel. It's the Broyhill Inn on Blowing Rock Road."

"OK, I can get there around eleven. Is that good for you?"

"That's just fine." she said. Then added in a low voice, "I can't wait to see you."

"Me too. Bye."

As soon as I hung up with Lindsey, I put in a call to York Minster and got Officer Frank Worthington on the phone.

"Any word on the case?" asked the Minster Policeman. "Hugh said you might have a lead."

"I might. I wonder if you could look at a picture for me and tell me if you recognize the person."

"If I can. Do you want to fax it?"

"I'll e-mail it, if that's all right."

"I'm at the computer now. The address is frankw@york-minster.org. I'll get it in a few moments."

"It's on the way," I said, as I hit the send button. "I'll call you back in about five minutes."

"I'll be here."

I went to the kitchen and got another cup of coffee, all the while thinking about how to handle the Lindsey Fodor problem.

After a few minutes, I went back to the phone and placed another call to the Minster.

"Did you get it?" I asked Frank when he came on the line.

"Just came in."

"And do you recognize the person?"

"I've seen her before. I just can't remember where. Should I know her?"

"I think you may have met her. I wonder if Kris Toth..."

"That's it!" he interrupted. "Kris' cousin. She introduced me. Said she was over here visiting."

"That's what I needed to know. Thanks."

Marilyn was sitting at her desk, as usual, doing the work of the church when I sauntered in.

"You look positively gluttonous with self-approbation," she said.

"Huh?"

She laughed. "I heard that line in a Hitchcock movie the other night. I've been waiting all week to use it on you."

I nodded. "It's a good one and I accept the compliment."

"You mean it's a compliment? I take it back then."

"Are there any heretical changes in the service I should know about before this evening?"

"Nope." She shook her head and held the bulletin up for me to look at. "Everything seems to be back to normal. Wenceslas will be verging though."

"That's fine. If we have to have a verger, he's the one to have. At least he has some credibility."

"Father Barna gave me his sermon title for Easter and

disappeared. He said he'd be back around six this evening."

"That's probably good. These two services can take care of themselves. Father Tony will be here as well to help celebrate. Are all the lay-readers lined up?"

"Ready to go. I called them myself. Brenda's been in a bit of a twirl."

"I can imagine."

Marilyn's voice dropped to a whisper although there was no one else in the office. "Word has it that she's looking at a position in another church."

"It will be our loss," I said somberly. "How about the Altar Guild?"

"The FOOSCHWAG members wouldn't have anything to do with the service, but the old Altar Guild members have stepped in for the stripping of the altar and Easter Sunday. I called them all this morning. They'll be here."

"That's great. Thanks."

I pulled up to the Broyhill Inn right at eleven o'clock. I parked my truck, went into the lobby and spotted Lindsey right away sitting in an armchair drinking a cup of coffee. She smiled as she saw me come in, put the cup of coffee down on the table next to her and greeted me with a hug and one of those kisses that made me wish – however briefly – that I was unattached.

"I'm glad you could make it," she said coyly, trying hard to blush. "Would you like to come up to my room?"

"I'd better not, Lindsey. Why don't you finish that cup of coffee? I'll get a cup and join you."

"OK." She looked quite taken aback, but returned to her chair.

I got a cup at the coffee station and joined her in the sitting area. I looked at her intently. She had gone from a self-assured temptress to a bundle of nerves in ninety seconds.

"I thought you wanted to see me," she said in a quiet voice.

"I did want to see you. There are a whole lot of things I'd like to clear up."

"I don't have to answer your questions."

"That's true, you don't. But I'm liable to be a whole lot more sympathetic than the York Police Authority. And let me assure you that extradition for murder is not a problem."

Lindsey was quiet for a long moment. "I'm not a murderer."

"I thought you might say that. I haven't decided if I believe you. You certainly haven't been honest with me."

"That's true. I haven't. How did you know?"

"I had a suspicion. The pills that you took on the plane. Aldactone. They're not prescribed for high blood pressure anymore. They're for hirsutism. And it runs in families. Kris had it."

She nodded her head. "I have it, too."

"You know that I went to see Kris' mother yesterday."

"I know. She told me. She also said that she didn't tell you anything."

"She didn't. Not much anyway. I did see a picture though. It was in the bathroom. A family picture with Kris and her mother, Wenceslas and guess who else?"

"Yes, well..."

"I'd like to get this cleared up."

"I didn't kill Kris. She was my cousin. I loved her."

I nodded and waited for her to continue.

"I'd like to call my grandfather. He should be here."

"Why don't we go down to the church? We can talk to him there."

Chapter 19

Kit and I flopped into the flivver and headed for the circus. These clowns were after the bishop. With the bishop dead, the Ministry of Clowns would be safe--at least for another three years. If I could get to Uncle Winky before he got to the bishop, I could save everyone a lot of trouble.

"Draw your heater," I said. "And get ready. These clowns ain't playin' patty-cake."

We went into the clown tent like a couple of turkeys into a Holiday Inn Thanksgiving Smorgesboard. Suddenly the lights came up, and we were surrounded. They were all there. Mr. Pickles, Tonk-Tonk, Grabby, Cheezo, Honker and Uncle Winky. Six clowns, two of us, eight guns, forty-eight bullets. Add it all up and you get sixty-four, which was the exact number of stogies I had smoked since Tuesday. I took it as a sign.

"Glad you're here, loogan," said Cheezo. "We been waitin' for you."

"I've got information for you boys," I said, grinning like a poached possum on a platter of parsnips. "I can help you sink the bishop's anti-clown agenda faster than a chicken-wire row-boat. But I want something from you."

"What's that?"

"You gotta back off. Take out the bishop and let everything else go."

"Depends on what you got, shoefly," said Tonk-Tonk.

"I've got just what you need," I said with a smile. Then I lit another cigar.

Lindsey and I found Wenceslas in the church. He was sitting in the front pew, looking at the Resurrection Window in the front of the church, his hands folded in his lap.

"Grandfather," said Lindsey in a quiet voice, giving him a kiss on the cheek.

"Hello, child," said Wenceslas with a smile and then nodded to me. "I suppose it is time."

"Yes sir, it is," I said.

"May we talk here?"

"It's as good a place as any."

"How much do you already know?"

"I know that Kris Toth was part of your family. I know that Lindsey, Emil and Jelly Barna, and Joseph Meyer are part of your family. I know that Kris was planning on stealing the diamond from the chalice in the York Minster treasury and that she was also planning to steal the cross belonging to Nicholas II. I know that she made a deal with a Minster Policeman named Alex Benwick to help her get into the treasury, but was killed before she could get away. That's what I know. Here's what I surmise."

Wenceslas and Lindsey looked at me, no expression on either face.

"When the article appeared in the paper saying that I was going to be helping the English police with the investigation, someone, probably you, Wenceslas, arranged for Father Barna to be assigned to the church."

Wenceslas nodded. "It was a happy coincidence that he had just become a priest. He is my sister's stepson, but he is an idiot. I hinted to the bishop that I would make a substantial contribution to the summer conference center if Emil could receive this interim appointment. The bishop said that he could not see the harm."

"All this so you could keep an eye on me and see if I discovered the whereabouts of the diamond. It was the same reason Lindsey joined me on the airplane. It would have been easy to find out which flight I was on and book a first class seat. The plane wasn't at all full."

"I don't know why Peppermint the Clown showed up. It's really the only thing that doesn't make sense."

"That idiot priest wanted to have a clown service," said Wenceslas. "I needed to go to Hungary and I thought that Joseph could keep an eye on him while I was gone." He sighed deeply. "I don't know why he was killed."

"If it's any consolation," I said, "I believe his death was an accident – or at least a series of unfortunate events. He had emphysema, a pnumothorax and heart arrhythmia. We think that Peppermint was trying to blow up that balloon when he saw the snakes, panicked and inhaled the balloon. The air rushed into his weakened lungs and ruptured some of the alveoli – the air sacs – and the surrounding capillaries. He couldn't breathe and rushed headlong into the sacristy where he had a heart attack almost immediately. Once one thing went wrong, everything snowballed. I am sorry."

Wenceslas nodded sadly.

"I also believe," I continued, "that in 1918, the Kaszas Imperial Circus had its last performance in Yekaterinburg. I also think that someone connected with the circus was present at the assassination of the Czar and his family."

Wenceslas sat up straight, his blue eyes registering unbelief. "How did you find this?"

"The legend holds that the women shot that day had sewn jewels into their clothes to keep them from the Bolsheviks. The assassins took these jewels once their gruesome work was accomplished. I think the York diamond was one of those jewels. And I also think the cross came out of Russia with the diamond."

"I don't know why the diamond and the cross were given to the Minster, but there they remained – undisturbed – for seventy-five years. Now we have a conspiracy to steal both items. I don't know the reason, but I suspect that the motive isn't money."

"You will not understand," said Wenceslas. "It is not part of your culture...your beliefs."

"I can try," I said, waiting.

"My father was at Yekaterinburg." Weceslas paused and looked up at the stained-glass window, as if making sure that all of his story was still with him.

"He was a dwarf as well, but taller than I am and very strong. He was an acrobat and would also perform feats of great strength." Wenceslas broke his concentration and looked at me with bright eyes. "He could bend an iron bar behind his head."

I nooded but didn't comment.

"This is the story that he told to us. The story of the diamond and the cross."

I looked at Lindsey. She was watching her grandfather, but I could tell she had heard this story before.

"My father was speaking with the Czar when the Bolsheviks came for them," Wceslas continued. "He watched the Bolsheviks place the family in a line and shoot them – all except the girl and a young boy who were taken away. When the Bolsheviks had finished their terrible work, my father and several of the performers were required to help place the bodies into a mine shaft. Afterwards, those performers were shot as well and left in the mine with the royal family and their entourage. But they did not go quietly. In the deadly struggle, two of the Bolsheviks were killed. My father, in the confusion, hid in a crevice and escaped execution. Then, when the cowards had gone, he searched the bodies of the dead traitors and found the cross and the diamond."

"He made his way back to Budapest over the next year and with him came the diamond and the cross. He thought that this wealth could buy the circus back – restore it to its former glory. It was not to be."

The door to the sacristy opened and someone scuttled into the church. We didn't see who it was, but Wenceslas stopped speaking for a moment until we heard the door close again. Then he continued.

"From the moment that the diamond came to the Kaszas family, it brought with it nothing but sorrow. It has always been cursed. We tried to sell it. We could not. Finally, a meeting was called of all the remaining elders of the family. It was decided that the diamond and the cross should be given to a church – a church that would keep it safe until it could be returned. The church should be rich enough that it would never need to sell the jewel. There were two churches chosen, but it was to York that it was taken. My aunt, Belle Kaszas, was living in America and was very rich. It was determined that she should give it as a gift. It would not raise suspicions. But, again, the curse. She died soon after she came into possession of the diamond. Her friend finally delivered it."

Lindsey reached out and took her grandfather's hand. He smiled at her, and then continued.

"The curse that followed our family lifted once the diamond and the cross were delivered to York Minster. Then, about ten years ago, it began again. We feel...the family believes...that when the bodies of the Romanovs were exhumed and buried in St. Petersburg, the curse began again. The cross and the diamond cry out to be returned to the martyrs."

"So you made plans to take the treasures back from the Minster?" I asked.

"These last five years. I realize now that it was a mistake. Two more deaths...and for nothing."

"Do you know who killed Kris?" asked Lindsey.

I nodded.

"Can you tell us?"

I shook my head.

"And do you know where the diamond is?" asked Wenceslas, still hopeful.

"Yep. But it's going back to the Minster."

St. Barnabas had been almost magically returned to its pre-Lenten appearance. The altar was back in place. The water feature had disappeared. The paraments were red as was our tradition. We didn't need to worry about offending the ox. The pig was back home and the monkey had left the building.

The instrumentalists and the choir started arriving for the seven o'clock Maundy Thursday service at about 6:15. The altar guild was scurrying around with last minute adjustments; Father Tony was making sure that all was in order. Wenceslas was having a word with the acolytes. And conspicuous only by his absence was Father Emil Barna.

Father Tony was the celebrant and it was a beautiful service or perhaps just seemed so in contrast with all that had come before. Either way, I was proud of the choir and, as the service ended in silence and semi-darkness, we all walked out into the warm night air with a feeling of hope and expectation – finally looking forward to Easter.

"I *knew* she couldn't be trusted," said Megan, after I had told her about my afternoon. "Meeting you at the hotel! I could scratch her eyes out!"

"That's cute," I commented. "You being so jealous and all."

"You're just lucky you didn't go up to her room."

"Um...yes, I am. Very lucky."

"You didn't, did you?" she asked, her gray eyes narrowing.

"Of course not."

"Because you *know* I'll find out."

"I know that you will," I nodded, happy to agree.

"So you did?"

"No, no," I stammered. "I meant that I knew you'd find out if I did, so I didn't."

"You mean you wanted to? The only reason you didn't is because you knew I'd find out?"

"Do you smell something burning?" I asked. "I'd better check the kabobs."

"Bad news on Good Friday," said Malcolm Walker, making one of his semi-regular appearances at the Slab. "I just got a call from our woman applicant. She's withdrawn her name from consideration."

"Did she hear about our Feng Shui Altar Guild?" I asked, motioning for Malcolm to take a seat with one hand while balancing a forkful of scrambled eggs with the other.

"She did, yes," Malcolm chuckled, "but that wasn't the reason. She was offered a job teaching at Lenoir-Rhyne College starting in the fall. It's where her folks live."

"But the other fellow is still coming?"

"A week from today. By the way, have you seen Father Barna?"

"I haven't been up to the church today. He didn't show up for the service last night. I thought that a bit odd, if not refreshing."

"No one has seen him since yesterday morning. He came in and gave Marilyn his sermon title for Easter and disappeared.

I've alerted Tony, and he has a sermon ready for Sunday if he needs it. He was going to help with the service in any event."

Suddenly the glass door to the Slab banged open and Dave stuck his head in.

"Careful of that door," Noylene called out.

"Sorry," said Dave, perfunctorily. Then spotted me at the table. "Hayden, you'd better drive up to your house. Your silent alarm's going off."

"Call Nancy," I said, "and have her meet me there."

Chapter 20

The drive up to my place took a good twenty minutes. I had installed a burglar alarm at Megan's insistence. It worked off the phone system and rang in the St. Germaine police station. The problem was that half the time I was always forgetting to set it. This was one of the mornings I remembered. I had fed Baxter, put him outside to chase whatever wildlife he could scare up, punched in the code, locked the door and headed into town.

I drove up into the mountains, pulled into the long gravel drive and slowed down as I neared the house. I had the feeling that something was very wrong. There was a car by the back door. Through my windshield, I saw Archimedes sitting on a branch by the kitchen window, looking at the ground. I reached under the seat of the truck and took out a .38 revolver, then opened the glove compartment and removed a box of shells. I loaded the gun, left the box of shells on the seat and stuck the revolver in the back waistband of my jeans.

I got out of the truck, left the door ajar and walked to the back door. There, lying next to the kitchen steps was Baxter. He'd been shot, but was still alive, lying still, his eyes closed and his breathing regular. When I bent down and scratched his ears, Baxter's eyes opened and he raised his head. I could see that the wound was high on his shoulder and wasn't bleeding too much. Probably a small caliber bullet, and if I were any judge, he'd be just fine.

I eased the kitchen door open and walked gingerly inside, immediately noticing quite a ruckus coming from the den. As quietly as I could, I made my way through the house, hoping to catch the invader by surprise. As I pushed the door to the old cabin open, I saw that I hadn't surprised anyone. There, standing in a pile of my antique hymnals and prayerbooks, a small, 9mm automatic in her hand, was Jelly Barna.

"Where is it?" she snarled, looking even more unattractive than usual. Maybe it was the gun.

"Kris' prayerbook. I know you have it. I talked with Margot this morning."

"It's there on the shelf," I said, pointing to my collection. I had close to four-hundred hymnals, Bibles and prayerbooks printed anywhere from the sixteenth through the nineteenth centuries. It was almost impossible to tell them apart by looking at the spines. Most of the printing was faded and the leather binding worn. Jelly was standing in the middle of about fifty of the books, having rifled quickly through them before tossing them to the floor.

"Let me see your gun," Jelly said. "Or I'll kill you right now."

I reached behind my back and pulled my revolver from my waistband. I didn't have any doubt that Jelly would do exactly what she said.

"Slowly. Take it out with two fingers. You make one quick move and I'll take your head off. I only shot your dog in the shoulder because I love animals. You I won't mind killing."

I held my gun out with two fingers, privately cursing my stupidity. Nancy would never let me live this down. That is, if I lived at all.

"Toss it," commanded Jelly, her 9mm still aimed directly between my eyes. I tossed it onto the couch where it bounced and settled, infinitely inviting, but out of reach.

"Now," said Jelly, lowering her gun slightly and pointing it at my midsection. "I'm just curious. How did you know?"

I shrugged. "Kris was strangled by a pair of pantyhose. They weren't hers – she was wearing garters – so I figured the murderer was probably a woman. I e-mailed your picture over to the Minster Police. The one from the Feng Shui website. One of them recognized you as Kris' cousin from America. You knew what Kris was planning. It had been planned for years. But you're not from the Kaszas family. You had no interest in seeing the diamond returned. You wanted it for yourself, so you followed Kris into the treasury and killed her. But she had already hidden the diamond."

"It's in the prayerbook. It has to be."

"See for yourself," I said. "Second shelf from the top, third book from the left."

Jelly kicked some books aside and made her way to the end of the shelf, all the while keeping her gun trained on me. She pulled the volume down and quickly found the hollow place in the spine. It was, of course, empty.

"Where is it?" she said.

I shrugged.

"Don't you move a muscle," said a voice behind me. It was Nancy. "If you so much as blink, I'll drop you like a three-legged donkey on St. Swithen's day." I had to smile. Someone, at least, had been reading my work. Still, I didn't relish being in the middle of two angry and determined women, both of whom were brandishing loaded weapons.

"Just drop the gun, Jelly," I said. "It's over."

"Well, I guess I'd rather go to an American prison for killing you than an English prison for killing Kris," she said simply, her arm extending and her finger tightening on the trigger.

The sound of a gun blast filled the room.

Chapter 21

I poured myself a drink, lit a cigar, and put my
feet up on the desk. Another case was in the bag, and
I was feeling as clever as a weasel in a chicken
suit. I slammed back the booze in a single gulp.
Suddenly a shot rang out; a woman screamed, or maybe
it was just the hooch. The door opened and there she
was. Lilith. Lilith Hammerschmidt and her singing
snake, Rolf. And I was on the barking end of a forty-
five.

"You killed him. The first man I ever truly
loved," sobbed Lilith.

"Who's that, Lilith?"

"Race. Race Rankle. He was the only one who under-
stood me."

"I didn't kill him, Lilith. The clowns did. It's all
yesterday's news."

"You did it. And I know why. Before I contracted
leprosy and changed my name to Lilith, I was Evette
Nimue."

Now I remembered. Race Rankle's associate priest.
No, it didn't pay to go skinny-dipping with an associate priest carrying political ambitions, no matter how
attractive she is. I had soured the deal. When Evette
disappeared, Race made it his business to know mine.
He'd been blackmailing me for years. He found out
about the kickbacks I was receiving from the Methodists for information. Those Methodists always wanted to
stay one step ahead. But when I refused to go along
with his leper colony scheme, he was going to turn me
in. I had to kill him. But I still had questions.

"Lilith, why was he wearing an evening gown?"

"He wasn't like that. We were going to a costume party."

I didn't buy it, but I shrugged it off. What people wore was their own business.

"So what are you going to do now, Lilith? Shoot me?"

Tears welled in her eye. "I think I will."

She tried to pull the trigger, but the last of her remaining fingers dropped to the floor along with her Roscoe. She hit the carpet on all threes, scrambling for the gun. I opened my desk drawer, calmly pulled out my thirty-eight and plugged her where she was.

"Sorry, Lilith. I can't have you squealin' to the bishop."

"Take care of Rolf for me," she whispered as she fell lifeless to the floor.

I nodded and scooped up the snake. There was still time to enter the Bishop's Invitational Choral Tournament, and I knew a place where the hamsters ran free.

"He's going to be OK?" asked Megan.

"Baxter will be fine," I said. "The vet removed the bullet. There shouldn't be any complications. He'll be limping for a while though."

"Thank goodness."

"What about me? You're not even concerned about me?"

"You've got Nancy to take care of you. And it's a good thing, too. What were you thinking?"

"Well, obviously I made a couple of mistakes. I underestimated the culprit."

"I'll say. Is she going to make it? Not that I care. I hate that woman."

"She's in critical condition, but she should make it. Nancy doesn't miss."

"Well, I hope for Nancy's sake that Jelly pulls through. She doesn't need that on her conscience."

"I agree."

"And the diamond?" Meg asked.

"Down at the bank in the vault. The Minster is sending someone for it."

"You're so clever. What about the reward?"

"I gave it to the Minster music fund."

"What about Father Barna? Did they ever find him?"

"The police picked him up in Raleigh, but he's denying that he knew anything about his wife's plan."

Meg nodded. "I hope that you're getting Nancy a very nice early Christmas present."

"It's not even Easter yet."

"An Easter present then."

"I'll do it," I said. "What do you think? A motorcycle?"

"That should do it."

Postlude

Chapter 22

"Marilyn," I called. "How 'bout that Java?" I pulled my hat low over my eyes, lit a stogie and leafed through a hymnal. I needed four hymns for the third Sunday of Easter and they weren't exactly leaping off the page. Marilyn sauntered in, her hips swinging like Benny Goodman's rhythm section. She pursed her lips and placed a cup of joe on the corner of the desk.

"Rocki Pilates is here to see you," Marilyn purred. "She says to tell you she brought some watercress sandwiches."

"Marilyn," I grinned, "you're a peach. Now take the rest of the day off."

"With pleasure."

I clicked the 24 lb. bond out of the old typewriter and placed it face down on the stack of paper sitting beside the well-used machine. Then I switched off the antique green-shaded banker's light and called it a day. Lent was finally over and tomorrow was Easter.

About the Author

Mark Schweizer, in varying stages of his professional career, has been a waiter, a chef, an opera singer, a college professor, a choir director, a composer and a publisher. He is now entering the final stage of his mid-life crisis. In the first stage, he changed careers and bought a green Jeep. In the second stage, he wrote *The Alto Wore Tweed* and bought a red Jeep.

Donis, his long-suffering wife of 25 years, just hopes that whatever happens, there won't be another jeep involved.